MW01106974

Twisted Situations

One Friend's Wicked Plot

Donna Plata

ACKNOWLEDGMENTS

First and foremost, I would like to thank God for blessing me with the talent to write a book in the first place.

To my parents, Saundra and Mark, thank you for always being there for me and supporting me.

To my stepdad, Walker, you have always treated me and loved me as if I were your own; for that I am grateful.

To my in laws; Gerri and Michael, I appreciate you for accepting me as your daughter.

To my children and niece, Lavell, Michael JR, DeMarco, Mariya, and Camille, I love you all dearly; you've brought so much joy to my life.

To my loving husband, Mike, thank you for always being here for me and loving on me.

To my siblings, Shaun, Shante', Tia, Janise, Cortinque, Cherese, Mark, Dante, and De'Vante, y'all always hold me down.

Last, but not least, thank you to my editor, Yara Kaleemah. Thank you for bringing my book to life. Without her, my book wouldn't be as great as it is. I really appreciate what you've done.

Twisted Situations

One Friend's Wicked Plot

Donna Plata

Donna Plata

Chapter 1

The rhythm of Pat's favorite song caused her hips to sway back and forth as she placed a beautiful black dress across her bed. It was a warm summer night and the sun was just beginning to set outside of her window.

Pat was semi excited about the evening being as though she had gone on many dates before. They all started the same. A handsome guy would meet her at the door with a smile and perhaps a box of candies. They'd go to a nice restaurant and talk about their should'a, could'a, would haves. She would seem to be impressed but it would never be enough.

She shook her head and grabbed the bottle of body wash from her dresser. It would be okay to pretend to want to go out with a man and not be obsessing over Ken.

Ken and Pat dated for a little over a year until he broke her heart. Most would say that they were the ideal couple to envy. When they would go out he would always be a gentleman open doors, pull out chairs and get the check. Pat often spoke about seeing herself married to Ken, buying her dream house, and raising their children. What Pat didn't know at the time was that Ken was already doing that with his wife Angela and their two kids. It broke her heart to find out that the man she came to love after a long time had betrayed her heart and trust. She knew as a woman what she had to do. She would not be the cause of those children growing up without their father in the home because she was an only child raised by her mother. Her father had left them to be with another woman. She always felt that the other woman stole her father away.

As she put the finishing touches on Pat's cell phone rang and from the ringtone she knew it was her home girl Brandy.

"What's up, B?"

" Hey girl. What's up? You about ready?"

"Yeah, girl. I'm finishing up now. You know you can't rush perfection."

"True, true…' cause tonight I'm a walking piece of art. They ain't ready for it." Brandy sucked her teeth and the two of them shared a laugh.

"Have you talked to Sasha?" asked Pat.

"Earlier but she's supposed to meet us at the club. Well, I'm like ten minutes from your crib. I'll be pulling up shortly."

"Alright, B, see you when you get here." Pat hung up.

Brandy honked the horn just as Pat stepped onto the porch. She locked the door and held her keys in her hand

"Damn, girl." Pat snapped her teeth, knocking on the window of Brandy's black 300C. "Ain't nobody trying to car jack yo ass 'round here."

"Shut up," Brandy rolled down the window. "You riding with me or nah?"

"Hell no," Pat leaned into the window. "Cause y'all ass will fuck around and be drunk as hell." Pat shook her head. "I'm driving my car. I'll follow you."

A brisk air met them as they climbed from their cars at the curb. Handing the valet their keys, Pat and Brandy step toward the front of the crowded club. It was around eleven and the flashy club was already filled with sexy women and burly men. Pat looked around and then took a seat at the bar,

"How may I help you?" Carolyn, the bartender asked. "Rum and coke?" she smiled at Pat.

"You know me to well."

"And for you?" she asked Brandy.

"A martini."

"Sure."

Brandy stared out onto the dance floor, her eyes landing on a tall man dressed in a white linen suit. He was dripped in gold jewels and taking shots from a bottle of Cîroc. Brandy's eyes locked with his for a brief moment before she turned to Pat.

"Where in the hell is Sasha?"

"Girl, hell if I know." Pat shrugged, taking a sip of her drink.

"Let me text her ass."

Brandy pulled out her phone, pretending not to notice the man in all white coming toward them. She finished the text and sat the phone on the counter.

"Good evening, Pretty lady." He spoke.

Pat turned and looked him up and down. He looked decent. He was fine as hell and his voice was sexy. He smelled like nice cologne. He might have a job, Pat smirked.

"Hey." Brandy looked over her shoulder to see if she saw Sasha.

"You and your friend want to come join me?"

"Join you?" Pat intervened with a laugh. "No, we're waiting for our friend."

"Well, does this 'friend' have a yacht?" he asked.

"A yacht?" Brandy burst into laughter. "You own a yacht?"

"Yes and we're having an all-white party tonight."

"So what? You picking up attendees at the club? You men are so pathetic." Pat sipped her drink. "Would you just go?"

Then, Sasha sashayed toward them. Even weighed over two hundred pounds, Sasha was fierce. She was dressed in a hip hugging dress and a pair of six inch stilettos. Her shaved Mohawk was slayed and as usual her makeup was on point. She was one of those women who were motivated by staring and pointing. Pat was envious of her pride and confidence. Sasha was not ashamed of all the curves she was blessed with. The women exchanged hugs and kisses while Sasha called the bartender over.

"Let me get a long island ice tea and a basket of hot wings. I'm hungry as hell." Sasha told her, sitting down.

"Damn, girl. Didn't you just come from home?" Brandy asked.

"Bitch, if you must know," Sasha leaned in, "I just came from Damon house."

"Damon? Bitch, no!" Pat laughed. "You know you shouldn't be going over there."

"That dick," Sasha sucked in her lips and closed her eyes real tight, "that dick is something serious."

The three of them laughed at Sasha's expense. Beyoncé's "Single Ladies" pumped through the club and that was their cue to hit the dance floor. Pat only two stepped—that was all she knew how to do—while Sasha and Brandy were dancing like video vixens. From the corner of her eye though, Pat spotted a tall mug of hot chocolate.

This guy stood about 6'4 with muscular build and, brown sexy eyes big full lips and a smile to match. He was very welled dressed from head to toe as if he didn't belong here. The ladies were in awe as he stepped to the ladies and introduced himself but focused on Pat.

In a deep baritone he said, "What up, though? I'm G. I couldn't help but notice you on the dance floor. I've been checking you out most of the night but waited until the right time to approach you."

There she was in the middle of a crowded club with hot chocolate whipping into her nostrils but all she could think about was her low down dirty ex. She was staring at G and his mouth was moving but she couldn't hear anything he was saying.

"Oh" she blinked her big doe eyes and snapped her teeth, "and you thought now was the right time to make your move?"

"Ouch," G swallowed hard, "I hope I didn't offend you."

"Well, I'm sure you can see," Pat looked at Brandy and Sasha.

"Uh," G looked mildly confused.

Brandy damn neared pushed Pat out of the way, catching her breath to say, "Forgive my friend here. She's a lil new to the dating scene."

Pat rolled her eyes, knowing that her best friend was getting ready to pretend she was Hitch.

"I'm Brandy. This is Sasha and this lil feisty one here is my girl Patricia."

"Patricia. Patricia what a lovely name." Gerald smiled at her.

"I guess," Pat shrugged and sat down.

"Can I buy you a drink?"

"Nah, I'm fine," she waved her hand.

G was persistent, though. He slid into the booth next to Pat and put his arm around her shoulder. She tried to move away but he cuffed her chin in his hand.

"Don't be so mean, Ma." He whispered in her ear. "I'm one of the good guys."

Pat wanted to laugh but instead she licked her bottom lip and said, "Oh, really?"

"Yea," he smiled and then waved one of the working girls over. "Bring us a bottle of Cîroc."

"What flavor?" she asked.

"Don't matter." G replied.

"Oh shit!" Sasha giggled. "Nigga got a little Goon in him." Then, she looked at the waitress. "I'll have a bottle of Henny. I like my sizzle dark."

G glanced at her from across the table. "You a big girl, huh?"

Sasha stared at him for a moment. Was that a compliment or an insult? Her top lip rolled into a snarl.

"No," G shook his head. "I just meant that you a Henny type of girl."

"Oh okay." She rolled her eyes and snapped her teeth. She was fixing to give him an ass ripping he'd always remember.

They spent a few hours drinking and laughing but then, it was time to go home. G put his number in Pat's phone and then, slid from the booth.

"Catch y'all later. And don't forget to call me." He said to Pat. He disappeared into the crowd.

As the ladies started to walk towards the door they couldn't help but notice valet bringing around a silver Audi and opening the door for G. Pat just smiled as Brandy tapped her on the shoulder, "Looks like you got a good one."

The ladies all got their cars and headed home.

Should I call him or not? Pat thought as she stepped inside to her big empty house where there was nobody waiting for her to come in. She let out a small sigh, kicking off her shoes. He is fine and from the looks of it he has a couple of dollars. Not that it motivated her at all—she has her own money. It wouldn't hurt to have a dude who can take her to a fancy dinner every once in a while. Damn, Pat looked at G's number in her phone. She wanted to call him and tell him to drive that Silver Audi to her house. She wondered how his hands will feel wrapped around her waist, his lips on her neck. Her panties were getting wet. Call him—a voice was screaming in her head. It had been months since someone laid the pipe on her. She put her thumb over the 'CALL' button and contemplated if she should press it. No, she tossed the phone on the couch. He's going to think I'm some thot. She frowned. Her vagina was pounding though at the thought of him. She picked up the phone and pressed 'CALL'.

"Yo," G answered.

"Uh," Pat said into the phone. "It's Pat."

"Oh, what's up, Baby Girl? You made it home, huh?"

"Yea," she walked into the kitchen and poured a glass of wine.

His voice was sexy on the phone and her nipples were hard. She heard him talking but she was too busy picturing them on her bedroom floor.

"Hello?" G said.

Pat cleared her throat, taking a swig of the wine. "I'm sorry."

"What you falling to sleep?" he laughed.

"No…" she took another sip. "I was…."

G chuckled again and whispered, "Thinking about this dick."

Damn! Pat almost spat across the room. No, he didn't just read her like a book. She was drooling while she thought about the dick! He laughed at her again and she was getting ready to hang up but G said something.

"You wet?"

"Wet?" she pretended to be clueless.

"Put your finger in it and tell me if it's wet." He demanded.

Pat hesitated for a moment. She didn't have to put her finger in it to tell him that it was wet. Her panties were soaked. "It's wet." She responded.

"But you didn't touch it."

Pat looked down at the phone and then put it back to her ear. "What are you watching me or something?"

There was a slight silence on the phone. "No, but I know that you didn't touch it. If you did you would have moaned."

"And what makes you say that?"

"Go head, touch it."

Pat licked her lips. She slowly slid her hand into her panties and separated the lips of her vagina. One finger slid inside and she grunted into the phone. Suddenly, her finger was soaked.

"It's so wet."

"You want me?"

"Yes," Pat moaned.

"How bad?"

"From the front, back, and the side." Pat rested her head on the back of the couch.

Just as she was about to explode there was a beep on her phone. It was Brandy.

"Hold on. I have to take this." She clicked over. "Hello."

"Pat? What's wrong, huh?" Brandy asked.

"What?" Pat took her hand out of her pussy and sat up on the couch.

"You sound…Oh, never mind... I was just calling to make sure you got home safe."

"Yea," Pat caught her breath. "I'm about to go to bed. I have to work tomorrow."

"Oh, okay. Good night and tell G I said see him later." Brandy hung up before she could protest.

Pat rolled her eyes and clicked back over to G. "Sorry about that."

"It's cool. You were about to cum for me."

"It's past my bedtime."

"I guess I can let you off the hook this time." G told her. "Night."

"Night." Pat smiled and hung up.

She tossed the phone on the couch and hurried upstairs to the bathroom. Turning on the shower, she grabbed her sex toy and stripped. She couldn't wait to get that nut out.

Chapter 2

Pat slammed her hand on the ringing alarm. It was time for yet another day of work. She rolled out of bed with a feeling she hadn't had in a while. When she walked into the living room, she grabbed her phone off the couch and went into the kitchen to start the coffee pot.

There were two messages from G. One said, "Good Morning, beautiful," and the other was an invitation to lunch. Pat smiled and put the phone down on the counter.

It was bad enough he made her pussy jump; she wasn't about to answer his messages with a quick reply. After drinking her daily cup of coffee, she went to get ready for work. She had a long day ahead.

Meanwhile Brandy was going through a thang that she felt required the attention of her girlfriend. So she called up Pat.

"Hey girl what's up?"

"Paaaat!!!"

"B, what's wrong?"

"I'm supposed to be going out to lunch with Bo."

"So what's the problem?" Pat asked.

"I sort of told Eric that I'd go out with him too."

"B?"

"They both met up outside in my driveway."

"So what happen?"

"Girl I left them fools out there! I wasn't about to go out there and be caught in the middle of that mess."

"I know that won't happen again." They both laughed.

"What's up with you?"

"Heading into the office. I have to show a house this afternoon."

"On this beautiful day Patricia?"

"That's right girl! Houses aren't gonna sell themselves."

"You right about that and speaking of G..."

"Now who said anything about G? We were talking bout houses!"

"Well I just wanted to be nosey! So did he call you," asked B

"Yeah he called."

"Pat, stop playing! What he say? What happened?"

"Well we talked on the phone for what seemed like hours then we said goodnight, I took a shower and went to bed."

"Mmm hmm…" Brandy shook her head on the other end of the phone.

"What?"

"Nothing just saying mmm hmm that's all"

"Hold on."

It was Nicole, her assistant at her real estate company. "Hello."

"Hi Ms. Davis just calling to inform you that the Williams' had to reschedule their appointment for today."

"Okay thanks Nicole. If you have nothing else go ahead and take the rest of the day off."

With a shocked look on her face, Nicole hurriedly replies, "Oh Wow thanks Ms. Davis; you must really be in a good mood."

Pat smiles, "Yeah Nicole I am, enjoy your day."

"You do the same Ms. Davis."

"B?" Pat said.

"Yeah?"

"Ok. Now where were we?"

"We were talking bout that fine ass man you met at the club last night. You know the one who drives the silver Audi?

"No, you were talking I was just listening."

"Ha ha! Okay Ms. Thang so when are y'all going out?"

"He did ask me if I wanted to go to lunch today but…"

"But what? Girl you better gone on out with that man and give him some"

"Brandy."

"What? I was just saying you better take advantage of all that sexiness you know you ain't had none."

"Oh we got jokes now, huh, B? Ain't you the one who just had two fools going at it over you?"

Brandy was quiet and then, Pat's other end clicked again. She looked down to see that it was G. Damn, she thought.

"Hold on, B." Pat said.

"You're line sure is hot this morning. Who is it? That hunk of chocolate?" Brandy joked as Pat put her on hold again.

"Good morning, Pat and how are you today?"

She was smiling so hard that she couldn't fix her lips to reply.

"Hello?"

"Hi, yes, I'm here and my day just got better thanks for asking."

"Oh really? Because you didn't answer my text this morning."

"What text?"

"So now you going to act like you didn't get it."

"Hold on, G. Let me tell Brandy I will call her back."

"Yea, you do that." G said.

"Ok hold on alright?" Pat clicked her phone. "B, gotta call you back you done spoke his sexy ass up."

"It's still me lil lady." G laughed into the phone.

What the… Pat thought as she clicked the phone again.

"Hello," she said cautiously.

"Yea," Brandy answered and Pat exhaled.

"Girl… G ass on the other end and I thought I clicked over to talk to you. He heard me call him sexy."

"And what's wrong with that? The man is fine."

"Girl, shut up. I'ma call you later." Pat clicked over for the last time.

"So you think I'm sexy."

"Uh…" Pat was still embarrassed.

"It's okay. Back to my text, you coming with me to lunch or nah?"

"I would love to but…"

"But what?" He asked.

"I don't know…"

"I know you ain't bout to say you don't know me like that. We ain't in high school."

G had a point and her stomach was growling. She thought about watching his lips as he talked.

"Okay, yes I'll go."

"That's what I'm talking about. I love a woman that wears big girl drawls." G joked. "I'll pick you up at a quarter to."

Pat gave him the address to her office and they hung up. G's car was parked at the curb in front of her office at the exact time he told her he would be there. A punctual man—check—Pat thought as she locked the office door and dropped her keys into her Dooney and Bourke handbag. She put a little switch in her hips as she walked toward the car and pulled the passenger door open.

"Hey baby." G reached over and kissed her on the cheek.

"Hey, you." She smiled at him while he pulled off.

All she could think about was the size of him. These days she was so lonely, sex was the only thing she could think of sometimes. When she was with Ken she was getting it on the regular. Though, she was glad that he was out of her life she missed being with him.

She relaxed in her seat and let the music soothe her. She didn't want G to sense the tension. She wondered where he was taking her but she knew that it would be nice. He looked like the type to spend a hundred or better on one plate. Soon, he pulled his car into a garage. He stepped out of the car and walked around to open the door for her. As he pulled her from her seat, he kissed her hand. Then, he led her on a short walk.

A table for two was set up on the roof top of a tall building. A man was playing the piano in the corner while they took their seats. A waiter, dressed in a tuxedo, placed a shrimp cocktail and basket of biscuits on the table. He poured them each a glass of champagne and then, disappeared into the building.

"This is nice." Pat told G.

"I'm glad you like it. So tell me," he started, his hand on her thigh, "what do you do for a living?"

"I'm a real estate agent." She told him.

G looked surprised as he nodded his head. "Interesting."

They spent some time talking about their lives, their accomplishments, and ambitions. G told her that he was a consultant but she didn't believe him. He said he worked for an art buying company. What black man you know named G works for an art company? Pat listened to him though, and hoped that he was nothing like Ken had been. When their lunch was over he dropped her back off at the office. To say the least, Pat was intrigued by him.

Chapter 3

"Alright now," Sasha said into her headset. "That's the end of our session hope you tune in again." She closed the session and stood up from her desk.

"Whoa man am I tired? This water is calling my name. A quick shower, get dressed and hit the mall gotta find something sexy for tonight." She spoke out loud.

Then her phone rings.

"Hello?"

"What's up Sasha?"

"Oh, hey, Randy!" Sasha smiled.

Now Randy is the inside plug for all the hottest events.

"What you getting into Ma?"

"Nothing much bout to jump in the shower, what's up?"

"I was calling to let you know that I'm putting you and your girls on the VIP list for the Grand Opening tonight."

" Oh shit! That's what's up!" She exclaimed.

"Yea, see you tonight."

"Thanks boo!"

As Sasha starts to look through her closet her phone rings, again.

"Sasha on the line! Who's this?" she pressed the phone to her ear.

"Girl, you so dramatic." Brandy said on the other end.

"Hey, girl what's going on?"

"Bout to get dressed looking for something to put on"

"Shouldn't be hard you got clothes galore in your closet."

"Oh you got jokes, B?"

"I'm just saying I mean you should join the SA."

"What the hell is SA?"

"Hi my name is Sasha and I'm a shopaholic," mocked Brandy

"Anyway Ran called me and said he put us on the VIP list for tonight"

"Oh okay that's what's up. I gotta find something cute to wear."

"Me too."

"Alright well while you're getting ready I'm bout to swing by to pick you up."

"Ok, I'll see you when you get here, then."

As Pat walked into the house she checked her phone. There was a text from Brandy, saying that they were invited to Randy's Grand Opening. She wasn't really in the mood to go partying but she knew that Sasha would be upset if she didn't go with them to get the latest celebrity drama. Sasha worked as a radio show host so it was her business to be at every party in town. Pat thought about what she would wear as she poured herself a glass of wine and pulled her ponytail lose. She needed a few to unwind while she thought about her lunch date with G. That man was just too good to be true. As she reminisced though, her phone rang. Ken's name popped up and she was immediately disgusted. Why in the hell is he calling me? She frowned, hitting ignore. The phone rang again.

"Stop…" she started to curse Ken out, then she realized it was G. She answered the phone with a smile. "What's going on, Player?"

"Is that supposed to be you're 'bad girl' voice?"

Pat was caught off guard so she laughed. "No. Hey boo."

"Oh, I'm your boo now, huh?"

She was going to say yes. He was her boo thang but she wasn't about to act like a vulnerable little girl. They were just getting to know each other and for all she knew he could be just like Ken.

"Boy bye!" Pat spat.

"So what you getting into?"

"Oh nothing," she lied as she placed a skin tight dress down on her bed and pulled out a pair of shoes. "I'ma call you back later." She told him.

"Okay. Bye, beautiful." G hung up.

Pat tossed the phone on the bed and started to get dressed.

Brandy and Sasha pulled up at the club around 10. They stepped out of the car and Brandy handed the valet her keys.

"Girl, I am rocking this outfit them niggas is gone be all on me tonight as usual." Sasha ran her hands down her thick sides. "Have you heard from Pat yet?"

"She's going to meet us." Brandy told her.

"Oh okay cause I wanna enjoy my VIP seats plus I heard it was gone be some ballers up in there."

"It would be so nice to catch me one instead of these whack ass broke niggas I've been meeting," said B. "Don't get me wrong I got a squad of some hustlers, I just want a squad of these niggas getting dat bread." Brandy shrugs as she slaps fives with Sasha, "you know what I'm saying?"

"I heard that girl well tonight we're on the prowl."

"You are so silly I mean hey if you like it I love it."

Pat arrived at the club and pulled to valet. She thought to herself, damn this is a lot of people. She got her band and headed upstairs to the VIP section that was blocked off by a velvet rope.

"Heyyyy, girl!" Sasha hugs Pat. "Glad you could make it

"Man this party is slapping where we sitting?"

"Right over there. B went to the bathroom."

22

"Alright."

As Pat walked over to the table her hand is grabbed by a gentleman.

"What's up sexy?" He flashed a smile of gold teeth. "I know you must be here with your man cause your too damn fine to be in here alone."

Pat jerked her arm from him. "If you thought I was with my man why would you put your hands on me?"

The dude threw his hands up and backed away. "Iight, shorty."

Before B could get out of the crowded bathroom, she overheard a group of females talking. "Girl that nigga got money! He stacked for days. Shid I'm trying to get on tonight cause that nigga G is dat deal you feel me? You remember when he made it rain and bought out the bar girrrrrrl bye." The conversation was still going on while Brandy made her way past the long line of females trying to get in the lady's room. Finally meeting up with her girls, they all decide to hit the dance floor. As they proceeded to the stairs an entourage of people came up and to everyone's surprise in the middle of the crowd was G. He stopped and looked at Pat,

"I thought you were staying in tonight."

"Yea, me too. These heffas drug me out."

"Don't go too far." He winked and his posy followed him to the other side of the VIP section. Pat instantly got butterflies in the pit of her stomach. Seeing him like this threw Pat for a loop. As she thought to herself, I hope this isn't gone be another Ken type situation." The man standing in front of her wasn't the man she had went to lunch with. The man standing in front of her was a celebrity with groupies and buff ass niggas that could pass for body guards. With enough ice on that Disney could skate on it.

"Well gone do ya thang lil lady you know where I'll be when you ready to get at me." G said.

Brandy leans closer to her ear and said "Now I know who those bitches were talking bout."

"What bitches?" said Pat.

"When I was in the bathroom I overheard these heffas talking bout this guy name G having stacks for days and that he was ballin major. Shid one of them even said she was gone do whatever for him to leave with her."

Once again all eyes were on the three. Men and women watched as their bodies moved to every beat of *Pussy Don't Fail Me Now* by Missy Elliott. Pat knew that she had competition in the club so she had to put on a show and that she did. She ran her hands through her hair, down the back of her neck, down her shoulder, caressing her body making every man watching her stand at attention.

"Aww this my shit." yelled one of the girls. "All the single ladies! All the single ladies! All the single ladies! All the single ladies now put your hands up!"

Just as the ladies were feeling themselves a group of men approached to just stop and stare and wish for a second that they were going home with them. There were a lot of women in the club on the dance floor but none stood out like these. The groupies were giving attitude and evil stares. You could tell that the jealousy was thick in the room and they saw the way G was watching Pat's every move.

"Uh uh uh uh she ain't bout to come up in here and get my man!" said one of the groupies.

Sasha was in her own lil world. She thought she was Beyoncé that night, doing all her moves down to the booty hop. The guys bit their fists when she began to pop it and drop it like it was hot! After a few songs, they decided to head back upstairs to VIP. When they reached the table they were met by two muscle bound men. "Ladies if you don't mind, G would like for you to join him at his table."

The ladies looked at each and followed behind the men. As they entered another hallway T I's song "You Can Have Whatever You Like" came on and it was perfect for what was yet to come. Not only were they in VIP, now they were beyond expectations. Never did they think they would be in the hottest club mingling with the hottest crowd. They didn't think the night could get any better.

The ladies were in the VIP for the VIP's. People were dancing, eating, playing pool or just standing around. Some of the men and women looked like they were supermodels. There was shrimp, crab legs, steak and potatoes, a dessert table, a chocolate fountain with strawberries and an endless champagne fountain. "If I didn't know better I'd swear we were at someone's wedding reception," said B.

"Hell yeah," Sasha and Pat nodded in agreement.

"Hello gorgeous," G interrupted, placing his hand on the small of Pat's back.

"Hey, baby." She turned and kissed him on the neck. "You didn't tell me you were someone famous," Pat whispered; her moist lips brushing against his ear.

"You didn't ask." He looked at her with a mischievous smile.

"Damn, G. We didn't know you were banking like this." Brandy blurted in his direction.

He smirked and pulled away from Pat for a moment. "No, just enjoying the fruits of my labor."

"Literally," Sasha chimed, stuffing a chocolate dipped strawberry in her mouth.".

G showed them to the table. Pat sat snuggly under his arm as he ordered other people around. The lights twinkled in his eyes a bit when he looked at her. He was trying to impress her and it was working. She was still dazzled that she didn't know who he really was or what he had. In the distance she saw other half naked women glaring at them. She smiled, knowing that he was only trying to get into her pants. His hand had been on her thigh for most of the night and every once in a while, he leaned over and sniffed the side of her neck.

Pat looked down at her watch. It was now 2 am and way past her bed time. She yawned, looking in Brandy's direction.

"Aww," Brandy pouted. "The party was just getting started."

"I know but I've got to work in the morning." Pat told her.

"Stick with yo man you'll see bigger and better; trust what I tell you." G put his hand on hers.

"I'm sure but my firm won't run itself." Pat smiled, tucking her clutch under her arm. "Now, excuse me."

Of course Sasha and Brandy weren't ready to go. They thought they had snagged a few of G's friends. That was cool and all but Pat was leaving either way. She stood there, waiting for them to gather their things.

"So, when will I see you again?" G asked.

"You have my number."

Sasha slid from the booth, fixing her skirt and Brandy wasn't far behind. She hurriedly typed her number into the dude's phone that she had been talking to all night. They exchanged quick 'good byes'.

"Gerald you sure know how to put shit together." Sasha said. "Yeah I try to. I hope my guys took good care of y'all."

"Oh most definitely," B smiled.

The ladies were escorted to their cars while they were laughing and grabbing each other; feeling their liquor. The night ended well especially for Patricia who was really feeling herself. Gerald wasn't like all of the other dudes she had dated. She was surprised, though, that he hadn't told her that he was a star. He probably thought she was the gold digging type of chick. That was far from the truth though. She was a self-made woman. As she drove home all she could think about was Gerald. She wanted to feel him inside of her. Maybe it was the liquor but it didn't matter. She wanted to fuck him.

"Damn," she said aloud as she pulled into the drive way. "I should call his fine ass on over here." She turned off the car and grabbed her purse.

Shuffling through it she got her phone and scrolled to Gerald's number. She was about to tap the call button but she tossed the phone on the counter. She was not about to chase him all of a sudden. She liked being the mouse anyway.

Chapter 4

The next morning Pat started her regular routine. Got dressed and headed out for work. This time she stopped for coffee and donuts something that she usually sent Nicole to get. By the time she had reached her office she had just missed what would be the surprise of her life.

"Good morning, Nicole."

"Good morning, Ms. Davis." Nicole smiled, as Pat walked into her office.

She looked around to all corners of the room and in awe she called Nicole. "Uhm Nicole what is all this?"

"Well Ms. Davis a delivery guy came and said he needed a signature for a delivery so I signed for it. And once I did that bouquets of flowers, balloons, and edible arrangements came from everywhere."

"Everything is so beautiful," said Pat still at a loss for words.

"There was a card too I put it on your desk."

"Thank you Nicole," Pat sat down as Nicole exited the room and closed the door behind her.

Pat opened the card and it read, "Hope I'm not over doing it or scaring you away but I just wanted to brighten your day before it began, Gerald."

"OMG!!! I gotta call Brandy."

"Hello," Brandy answers.

"Girl you will never believe what Gerald did."

"Girl what?" Brandy asked with excitement in her voice.

"He sent me like ten dozen roses, a truck load of balloons and enough fruit to last me a week. It was so beautiful and thoughtful girl. I'm thinking like he can get it. This man is amazing."

"WOW!!! He must really like you, you sure you didn't give him some already?"

"Girl bye if he had some of this good good he wouldn't be sending me flowers he'd be sending me on vacation."

"I hear that girl, Pat hold on Sasha's clicking in I'm gone merge the call."

"Heeeey." They all sang.

"What's up Sasha?" Pat leaned back in her seat, waiting for some juicy drama.

"Girl you will never guess who I just ran into." She caught her breath.

"Who?" Brandy and Pat asked at the same time.

"Ken," Sasha exclaimed and there was a brief silence.

"Ken?" Patricia's eyebrows rose on her forehead.

Brandy snapped her teeth, "Well what happen?"

"Ugh he was going on and on about how he messed up, how he had to get Pat back. How he should've kept it real from day one no matter what. I know he's planning something because he was coming out the jewelry store with a box wrapped with a bow." Sasha told them.

"Hmm I wonder what that mean because it couldn't possibly mean what I'm thinking. Can't be." said ,Brandy "cause the nigga already married." She laughed. "Well, I hope he don't go over there and fuck with her head. It took so long for her to get over him. I would hate for all of her hard work go to waste".

"Plus she's got a new thang that is digging her" said Sasha.

"Right, he is so nice to her and in a short amount of time. My girl deserves to be happy not two timed by some lying ass, already married, no good for nothing, think he slick ole…"

"Y'all bitches sitting here talking like I ain't on the phone. And for the record, there is nothing Ken can do to get back with me. I got work to do so I'll holla at y'all later.' She hung up."

To say the least, Pat was uptight. She was mad as hell that she was sitting in her office, surrounded by gifts that Gerald had sent her, thinking about Ken. He has his chance, she shook her head and turned on her computer.

Her cell phone rang and it's a private call. She answers, "Hello," but the phone is silent, no voice, no noise, no nothing she hangs the phone up.

Next the office phone rings Nicole answers this time and Pat looks to see if she's going to tell her that it's for her or they hung up but she didn't. Pat continues going through her stack of papers but can't help but to stop and smell the roses. Literally, she smelled a bouquet of roses that were on her desk. *Well the least I can do is call and say thank you*, I mean don't want him to think I'm ungrateful.

The phone rings three times then a handsome voice said, "What's up lil lady?"

"Hello Gerald, nothing much I just wanted to call and say thank you for everything. I mean when I walked in my office my mouth dropped and I was in awe. That was so nice of you. I feel so special.

"You ought to feel special lil lady," said Gerald. "I told you I don't know what fool let a precious gem get away and slip through his fingers but his lost."

"Yeah it is." Pat said in a flirtatious voice. "Could you hold on I'm getting another call." She clicked over. "Hello?"

" Hey girl. What's up?" said Brandy.

"Talking to Gerald. What's up?"

"Well I don't wanna interrupt that conversation so call me later when you get a chance."

"Ok," She clicked over again. "Hello! Hello aww I hope he didn't hang up". Just then she heard that sexy voice that she was starting to get used to hearing.

"Hey lil lady I had to click over too, now where were we?"

"You were telling me how special I was and how glad you are that we met,"

"Well put, lil lady. I might not have said it but I damn sure was thinking it."

"Oh really," said Pat.

"Yea really wit yo sexy self."

Pat was grinning from ear to hear, "You think I'm sexy too?"

"Are you kidding? You must be kidding; you know you sexy as hell. I see the way all the fellas were on you at the club. Well lil lady I hate to cut it short, but I gotta shoot a couple moves so…"

"Oh no. No problem. I took up enough of your time as it is."

"Naw Ma, you can get all the time you want. Hit me up later. Maybe we can hook up if you're free."

"I sure will or you can call me when your done taking care of your business and get settled."

"Alright I'll holla at ya."

Beep, the intercom chimed.

"Ms. Davis?" Nicole said.

"Yes, Nicole."

"Is there anything else that you need me to do before I leave?"

Pat thought to herself, WOW I didn't know it was this late.

"No, Nicole. I'm good. In fact, I'm gonna head out with you. I lost track of time."

As she began to get her things together, her cell phone rang displaying private on the caller ID again. This time Pat sent it to voicemail. "People still play on the phone? I'm grown as hell. where they do that at?"

Making sure all the lights were off and the doors were locked the two women left and parted ways. Minutes before Pat reached her house, her cell phone rang again this time displaying a name across the screen; Kenneth Ross.

Since she had endured listening to Brandy and Sasha's conversation, she had anticipated a call from him. She looked at the phone, contemplating on whether or not to answer. A part of her needed to curse his ass out. He had left her high and dry. The other part of her couldn't stand the sound of his voice. The phone was still vibrating on the seat next to her. Shit, she thought and pressed the talk button.

"Hello," Pat answered with an attitude but at the same time trying to sound as if she wasn't still hurt.

"Hey, baby. It's me, Ken." There was a brief silence. "Don't hang up. Are you still there?"

Pat huffed into the phone, "Yeah, I'm here and I'm not your baby."

"Well, I mean you know it's a habit. I apologize. Listen, baby, I mean Patricia… could you please hear me out?"

"Hear you out about what Ken?"

"There's a lot that you don't know about the situation." He told me.

"A lot like what?" Pat snapped her teeth. She was tired of beating around the damn bush. "I know your married with kids. What else don't I know? I know you're a liar who played with me for over a year; a whole fuckin year Ken!"

Pat had to catch herself. She was getting teary eyed and wasn't about to give him the satisfaction of getting to her. "What is it that you want Ken?"

Ken took a deep breath, "Pat I want, no, I need to see you. It's very important."

"So is my time but you're wasting it," said Pat.

"Patricia, I'm not perfect, never said I was or tried to be. Just please give me a chance to explain."

Even with the feeling in the pit of her stomach, she had so much hatred towards Ken for hurting her. The voice in the back of her head was telling her to say no but she agreed to meet with him the next day.

Chapter 5

The next day things seemed like they were alright until Pat started receiving the private calls again. *Ugh not today who the hell still plays on the phone anyway where they do that at? Ugh, my mind is running crazy I mean I know how I'm supposed to feel and act towards him but there's a small part of me that wants to hear him out. I don't know why but...Uggghhh what the hell did I just do damnit!!!*

The doorbell rings. Pat tries to take her time to answer it. Although she agreed to meet with him she was in no rush to see him. Pat opens the door, dressed in a backless one piece with some stilettos; looking good and smelling good. Thinking to herself this nigga gone regret fucking up with this bitch.

"Come in," Pat said.

"Damn, Patricia, you look amazing," Ken tried to lean towards kissing her.

Pat pulled back and said, "Uhn uhn this ain't that. Say what you came to say. We ain't cool." She rolled her eyes.

"Man, I never thought we would be here," Ken said.

"Well neither did I, Cheater. Oops did I say that? My bad." She took a seat on the sofa.

"Patricia, you have every right to be mad."

Patricia began to yell, "You damn right I do! How the hell? Wait no, I said I wasn't gonna do this." She tried to calm herself down. "Just say what you gotta say so we can get this over with."

"Patricia, listen when I met you my marriage was falling apart. It had fell apart. There was no saving it whatsoever, no reconciling. No staying together for the kids none of that. She couldn't accept the fact that it was over and I was moving on. I had filed for divorce but she would never sign the papers so legally I'm still married but..."

"Ken, there is no but," she was about to tear him a new one.

"Wait let me finish." Pat sits back and folds her arms so he continues.

"Yes, legally I'm still married but I haven't been in that marriage with her in years. I made sure it was over before I moved on so that there wouldn't be any mixed feelings or thoughts of regret. Hell babe you even been to my crib spent many of nights now come on. Babe when I met you I was the happiest I had ever been in a long time. You know how good we were together inseparable. I wouldn't do anything to hurt you; babe you know that."

"Oh I know that? I guess these are tears of joy on my face. I guess my heart got broken on its own. I've been hurting all of this time, asking myself how, I mean, why. What did I do wrong?"

"Baby" Ken knelt on the floor in front of her, "No, no baby you did nothing wrong." He told her, wiping the tears from her face and looking into her eyes he leans in to kiss her. She is so caught in the moment that she kisses him back. And with every kiss he said he's sorry. He's kissing her lips nose forehead and cheeks and each time he apologizes. "Baby I'm sorry for hurting you," and he holds her in his arms as she cried harder. "Baby, I'm sorry. Let me make it up to you and show you how sorry I am."

Just then his cell phone rings and he ignores it. Then Pat's cell phone rings and when she looks at it the caller ID said private. Then his phone rings again and he hits ignore saying he doesn't want anyone to disturb him. The phones kept ringing one after the other but she didn't peep the connection.

She got up went into the bathroom, fixed herself up and changed her whole attitude. Pat looked in the mirror and saw that hurt woman who was broken down and felt lifeless. Until she realized how far she's come to get to where she's at, over him. "Alright I almost fell for it."

"Almost fell for what Pat?"

"The okie doke. That's what. I'm not a fool! I'm not falling for no more of your games. What's up? Have you said all you needed to say?"

"Pat I thought…"

"You thought what? That you'd come here tell me a few bullshitting ass lies and we'd kiss and make up? Get the fuck outta here with that bullshit."

"Patricia I'm telling you the truth. What else you want me to do?"

"Uhm now that you mentioned it, I need you to leave."

"What?" He looked at her with a shocked look on his face.

"You heard me get up and go on. I need time to think about all of this." She told him.

"Alright, that's real. Well you take all the time you want I'll be here waiting for you."

Pat leans with her head against the door as she closes it behind Ken.

Her phone rings "Oh hell yeah! I'm bout to cuss somebody the hell out!" Pat said as she runs to the phone. Just as she gets to it they hang up and it was a missed call from Gerald. She didn't call him right back, though. She had to call up her girl and tell her what happened.

"Hey Brandy."

"What's the deal?"

"I cried and gave in and I feel like such a fool."

"Wait! What?"

"I had my mad face on then I got all sentimental and got to crying and shit."

"Pat I'm trying to listen and everything but I don't have a clue what you're talking about."

"Oh my bad girl I agreed to let Ken come over and…"

"You slept with him?"

"Hell no" yelled Pat.

"Oh I was about to say. Well, what did he have to say for his self?"

"That he and his wife weren't together. He loved me…blah blah blah. I mean I was hearing all of that and a part of me just wanted to just lay in his arms and let him tell me everything was gonna be ok. Then the other part wanted to stay mad at him, you get what I'm saying?"

"Yeah girl you still love him! Y'all just going through some things" Brandy said. "Pat listen, please whatever you decide to do let it be because that's what you want to do not cause it's what you wanna hear or cause of what someone else wants you to do. If you do decide to take him back, don't be so quick to count the wife out. There's still a lot of unanswered questions you need to know."

"Thanks Brandy. I'm just like once I started getting over him I meet this incredible man and things are going good and now this."

"No, Pat listen to me don't throw what you have for Gerald away. You keep enjoying yourself with him. Letting him treat you like your supposed to be treated and all else will fall into place".

"With that being said I'm gone go in here and take me a nice hot steamy shower and lay it down. I'll talk to you later love ya girl."

"Love ya back."

Chapter 6

Pat tossed and turned thinking of how everything was unraveling when she woke up from the ringing of her alarm clock. Her pillow was drenched with sweat. "Man those were more like nightmares; *oh my goodness*". As she gets out the bed her phone starts ringing. "Who could this be this early in the morning?" Private call was across the screen again so she ignored it. *"Too early for this bullshit. I need to clear my head I think I'm going to take the day off or go in late. Yup that's what I'm doing gotta get my head right"*. She goes to the bathroom and got back in the bed. Pat is awakened by knocking at the door. She gets up to see who it is and it's Sasha and Brandy. She opens the door.

"Hey y'all. What's up?"

"Well, hell we've only been calling your ass since forever got everybody worried." said Brandy.

"Right and I done left my hair appointment so you know we was worried." said Sasha.

"I'm fine you guys just needed some time to myself that's all".

"Well that's fine and dandy but next time can you let a sista know or something?"

"Now what's up? What got you stuck up in the crib missing work?" Asks B.

"I had to get my thoughts together about Ken before I could do anything with Gerald."

"Alright so have you done that?" Sasha asked as she looked through the refrigerator.

"Yes," replied Pat.

"Cause I'm just saying if you don't want him I'll take him off your hands," Brandy twirled her fingernails.

"Brandy?" Sasha gasped.

"What? I'm just saying. You know, I'm just teasing."

"Uhm huh let me get myself together." She told her friends.

Later on that night Pat decides to give Gerald a call. "I've ignored his sexy ass for way too long and I'm not letting a good one get away. Ooh the phone is ringing I'm so nervous like this is my first time calling. Damn voicemail well makes it a good one." (Beep)

"Hi, Gerald. This is Pat, sorry I didn't call you back earlier. I had a lot on my mind so when you get a chance gimme a call bye."

I hope I did not mess this up because I will kick my own ass." As Pat gets comfortable on the couch she watches the movie for all of about an hour and a half before she dozes off. About a half hour later around 9:30p her phone rings and she's startled by it. She answers clearing her throat.

"Uh huh, hello."

"How ya doing lil lady?"

"Hey I'm doing a lot better. Thanks for asking. Gerald I want to explain why it took so long to return your call."

Gerald interrupts, "You don't have to explain a thing."

Pat insists that she wants him to know.

"Well I want you to know just in case. Who knows maybe we'll continue talking months from now and I just don't want this to be an issue or whatever. I mean this is the deal I let my ex come over and we got a lot off of our chest and since then I've been, well I don't wanna say lost but maybe indecisive. I just didn't wanna start or pursue anything until I got this taken care of. You are a wonderful man and I didn't want to bring old luggage into our new friendship."

"That's real and I respect you more for that. I told you from day one I sit back and wait then play my position. I knew you'd call eventually. I made it hard to stay off your mind."

"Oh is that right?"

"Yeah I'm gone make you a believer you watch and see."

"Low key, I believe you now because you played a big part in my decision making on not taking Ken back."

"Ahh okay okay so in other words you feeling a nigga huh? Ain't nothing wrong with that. Just let whateva gone happens happen it can be a beautiful thing or a missed opportunity. The choice is yours."

Pat blushes, "You always say something sweet and sincere to make me cheese hard as hell."

"You need to smile and keep one on that gorgeous face of yours."

Pat thinks about it and asks, "Gerald, when are we going out again?"

"Whenever your free. I can always make arrangements to be with you. The question is are you ready to give in and be happy, live for the moment not tomorrow?"

"Uhm as a matter of fact I am. I was just telling B that earlier," said Pat.

"Alright then. Well what's up for the weekend you made any plans yet?"

"None so far" she said excited to hear what comes next.

"Well don't this weekend I got you."

"Well I gotta make a few calls really quick and I'll give you a call tomorrow."

"Okay, I'll be looking forward to it."

The day seemed so bright, sunny, and full of opportunity. The summer air was filled with smoke smells from barbeque pits. Kids were outside riding their bikes, getting wet with the sprinklers, just enjoying being a kid. As Pat sat outside on her porch drinking a glass of iced tea she felt like a kid herself on the inside. She was anxiously awaiting a phone call from Gerald to see what her weekend would consist of.

"Hey Ms. Lady," Pat turns and looks around. It was Ms. Watson from across the street. "How you doing Ms. Lady?

Haven't seen you out front in a lil while. What's going on?"

"Hey I'm fine. How you doing Ms. Watson?"

"Oh shoot Ms. Watson is doing really good Suga, just taking it easy since my falling."

With a shocked look of concern on her face Pat said, "OMG!!! Are you ok? Do you need to sit down?"

"Now, don't make a fuss over me. I'm fine. Doctors said I was a natural healer. I slipped down the last couple stairs and bruised my tail bone but no broken bones. No surgeries so I'm fine."

"Well that's good Ms. Watson. Glad to hear you're doing better."

"Yes, Pat. I was just coming over to ask you a question. Now you know I don't like to get involved in other people's business, you know that."

Pat mumbles, "Uhm huh…I know you don't Ms. Watson but what's up?"

"Well every night around 11:30 I see a man stand outside your window dressed in black."

"A man outside my window," Pat said as her heart began to race.

"Yes and once you turn off you're lights he leaves. I hardly see you so I could never tell you but I believe it was that nice gentleman you use to date but I'm not for sure."

"Well thank you Ms. Watson. I'm gone have to look further into this."

"Your welcome suga. I'm gone keep an eye out next time I'll call the police."

Pat is uneased now that she has learned that a man has been creeping around her house late night hours. The thought of Ken being the guy peeping through her window was unsettling to her. Just as she began to drift into the what if's her phone rang and startled her.

"Hello," she answered with a cracked voice.

By the sound of her voice Gerald knew something was up.

"What's the matter lil lady?"

Clearing her throat, Pat replied, "A neighbor of mine just told me that every night she sees a man dressed in black outside my window until I turn my lights off. I can't think of anyone else but Ken and if it is him I'm gone cuss his ass out but if it's not…"

She lets out a small sigh and Gerald hears it.

"Don't worry. I'm gone take care of it let me call you right back."

About forty-five minutes go past then Pat hears a knock on the door. "Who is it?" She asked before opening the door.

"Hi my name is Robert and I'm with Steele Security ma'am we were sent by Mr. Briggs to install a security system."

She opens the door and there were two men waiting on the porch and going back and forth to the truck to get equipment.

"Hello ma'am we're supposed to be hooking up a security system for you today."

"Oh I had no idea so where do you need to start at?"

"Well we can start in the living room. We have motion detectors, cameras, and an alarm system. That goes straight to the police and the fire department in case of an emergency. We will be done as soon as possible; approximately forty-five minutes to an hour."

"Thank you. Take your time my name is Patricia if you need anything."

Patricia heads to her bedroom and closes the door behind her and pulls out her cell phone. The phone rings and a voice picks up.

"What's up lil lady?"

"Man you are full of surprises, huh? I really appreciate what you did I mean I…"

" I know it's only been a short while but if I can do anything to make you feel safe and secure I'm gone do it. I told you I'm really feeling you."

"Well they're hooking everything up right now as we speak I had to call and thank you."

"No problem."

"Oh for this you gotta let me take you out."

"You wanna take yo manz out? That's what's up. You just let me know when."

"Alright I sure will and I can't wait until this weekend either. Hey you never told me where we were going"

"Remember live for today and not for tomorrow."

"I remember." She said with a smile.

"Well let me know after everything is hooked up, they show you how to work it and everybody is gone," said Gerald.

"Ok I will and thank you again MUAH!!!"

As she hung up the phone there was a knock on her bedroom door.

"Coming," Pat opens the door.

"Okay let me show you how everything works."

After all the men had left and Pat picked up the mess that was left behind. She decided to pour herself a glass of wine and chill out across the couch.

Chapter 7

Brandy was just getting in from a date with Daniel, a fine fireman that she had met. She was still floating cause he was so romantic she didn't even want the date to end.

Ahh Daniel, I can't wait until the next time I see your sexy ass you just might get it. Welp let me heat my food back up and relax from a well-deserved evening.

Over on Sasha's end she was enjoying her time with a quart size iced cold strawberry cheesecake ice cream. There is nothing better than after a long day of work diving into some Cold Stone Ice cream mmm my favorite.

Damn the weekend had arrived quickly. Pat turned off the alarm clock and sat up in bed. It was finally Friday and her weekend away with Gerald was right around the corner. She looks in the mirror and said, "Just one more day. Just one more day!"

OMG I'm so excited nervous but excited at the same time. Well let me get ready for work. Heading out she puts her new security code into the key pad and starts her day.

On her way to work Pat's cell phone rings again private is displayed across the screen she hits ignore and throws it in her purse. She arrives at work at 9:15 a.m. and is greeted by Nicole.

"Good morning, Ms. Davis. Before you go into your office a package was delivered here this morning."

"Thank you Nicole she takes the package and goes into her office to get situated."

She opens the envelope and pulls out a key card and a lil note attached.

"What's up lil lady? Here's your key card for the room. I got two rooms so you wouldn't think I was trying to rush things between us. I will meet you up there around check-in time see ya later, Gerald."

That guy is full of surprises but little do he know depending on how this weekend goes he might be getting some of this good good.

44

'Nicole, could you clear my schedule for today? I've got some running around to do."

"Yes, ma'am I sure will."

"Thanks. I gotta go find me something to wear. What time is it?" Pat asked as she looks at her watch 9:30 a.m. Perfect have some breakfast manicure and pedicure then hit the mall.

"See ya later, Nicole."

"Bye, Ms. Davis,"

Then, her phone rang as she climbed into her car. "What's up, B?"

"Hey girl you got a minute? You at work?"

"Yes and no I took the rest of the day off to get ready for tomorrow."

"Oh that's right how could I forget about tomorrow?" Brandy asked with a sarcastic tone. "So what are you taking with you besides your toothbrush?"

"Ha-ha somebody's full of jokes this morning huh? And to answer your question nothing."

"NASTY!!"

"Well you asked, actually I'm on my way right now to get breakfast mani and pedi and hit the mall you wanna come with?"

"Let me think ahh… sike nah yeah you picking me up?"

"Yeah, I'll come scoop you, you ready?"

"I will be by the time you get here."

"Alright see you in a minute then."

"Okay."

Pat is jamming to the sounds of Anthony Hamilton and soon reaches Brandy's house. Brandy comes out and gets in the car.

"What's up girl?" Brandy asks as Pat turns down the music

"Nothing. Look, Gerald sent me the hotel key through fed-ex and told me he'd meet me there."

"So what's the problem?"

"I don't know. He got two rooms said he didn't want me to think he was rushing anything."

"Ok what did you want to share a room with him?"

"No, yeah. I don't know. I guess I just don't know what to expect from him or what he expects from me."

"Well apparently he only expects time from you so far," said Brandy. "Now afterwards is a different story."

"Yeah I guess I just want everything to go right. That's all. It's been so long"

"Pat listen don't think too much about this just go and enjoy yourself. Whatever happens or doesn't happen just have fun."

"Yeah your right." As the pair get out the car Brandy's cell phone rings.

"Hello."

"Hello Auntie B you got a minute?"

"Yeah Char what's up?"

It was her niece, Charlene—who was a problem child for her sister but never gave her any trouble.

"Well, mama put me out. She said I had to find somewhere to go. I can't stay here anymore."

"And why did she say this?"

"I don't know, well cause I'm causing problems between her and Rick."

"Rick?" said Brandy.

"Yeah her new boyfriend but auntie I swear I haven't been doing nothing. It's like every time she gets a new man she wants me to leave. So can I come chill with you for a while?"

"Uhm yeah sure Char. Let me call you back. I'm out with Patricia right now. I'm gone find out what's what with your mom then I'll get back with you."

"Ok, love you auntie."

"Love you too Char."

"What's wrong Brandy?" Pat asks.

"Charlene said that my sister put her out and she wants to come stay with me for a while," she poked her lip out, "but I like my space." Brandy shook her head. "Oh well let's not dwell on this. We came here to find you something freaky for your weekend." An hour goes by and the ladies are satisfied with the choices made.

"Girl he is gone be tripping when he sees you in that teddy."

"I hope so it's only been a few weeks I'm not trying to rush or anything but damn a sista do get lonely at night."

"You ain't got to tell me you wanna be laid up in those milk chocolate strong arms cuddled up in bed butt naked listening to Teddy Pendergrass."

"You so silly but that would be nice."

"Then go for it Pat you don't have to marry the nigga. I mean unless somewhere down the line that comes up but allow yourself to be tempted and act on it if you want to. I know I would if I was you. I'm more excited than you are about spending the weekend with Gerald."

Chapter 8

After dropping Brandy off at home, Patricia started getting the private calls again. Oh wow really nope whoever you are you won't mess up my mood. Let me call my girl I ain't' heard from her. The phone rings "what up bitch? Damn you can't call nobody?" (in her pimp voice) what up?"

"Shit chillin waiting on my client to get here that's about it." Yeah I was just with B we hit the mall up to get a few things ya know."

"Yeah I know oh ok Pat my clients here let me call you back."

"Go head girl call me later."

"Ok."

Patricia heads home. As she approached her house a black on black Impala speeds from in front of her house.

"What the hell was that about?" said Pat.

Pat enters her security code on her alarm pad to gain entrance in her home. Just as pat opens the door her phone rings. She closes the door behind her then pulls her phone out of her purse.

"Hello, hey lil lady what's up? Sounds like something is wrong.".

"I'm bout to call and cuss Ken's ass out for stalking my house."

"Oh you seen him?"

"Naw somebody just sped from in front of my house. I mean who else could it be?"

"This nigga throwing me off my square maybe I need to holla at him for you."

"It's cool I ain't worried bout him anyway. I'm really looking forward to this weekend."

"Oh is that so? All that means is I better make it count."

"I'm sure you will you always do."

"Thanks I try. Well I'm not gone hold you. I'll call you in a lil while alright?"

As soon as Pat ends her call with Gerald her phone rings with private across the screen. Pat answers hello with an attitude hello she hears nothing then hangs up. "Damn whoever the hell that is, is working my last nerves". Pat thought about calling the phone company. She wanted these messages to stop. Although, she was almost sure it was Kenneth. She would have called and cussed his ass out but she wasn't about to ruin her weekend with Gerald.

As she gathered her stuff for the weekend, she called Brandy.

"Hello." Brandy answered.

"Brandy I told you bout what Ms. Watson said right?"

"Yeah."

"Well tell me why I come home and this black Impala speeds from in front of my house."

"Oh hell naw did you see who was in it?"

"Naw the windows were tinted. I know it's Ken's ass. He probably sending somebody over here."

"Good it probably was his ass anyway oh trifling ass nigga ugh I can't stand him."

"I know right."

"Hold on Pat, my other line is ringing." Brandy told her

"Gone head, I'll call you back."

"OK, hello." Brandy spoke into her phone.

"Auntie B did you talk to my mama?" her niece asked.

"Yeah I did Char and from what she tells me you're being real disrespectful."

Brandy didn't have time to be playing games with her. She didn't want the young girl to think she could bamboozle her.

"Auntie B," Char whined into the phone.

"Hold on," Brandy cuts her off, "now you know I'm not gone play that with you right?"

"Yes but Auntie B…"

"Wait, Char let me finish you're gonna get a job that's first and foremost. And we're gonna get your life back on track cause this I don't care attitude gotta go."

"Auntie B I hear you but mama lying."

"Watch your mouth Char."

"I mean but she's only doing this because she got a new man and don't want me around. I told her that he looks at me funny and ever since then she been acting funny towards me. That's how it is with all the men she dates. Mom dresses down and I dress sexier I mean Auntie you know what I mean."

"Yeah Char I know what you mean. Well we'll go over all the ground rules when you get here. I mean I know your eighteen but there's only one adult in this house."

"I feel you Auntie love you and thank you."

"No problem Char that's what family is for."

Meanwhile Sasha was finishing up with her client and then her phone rang.

"Hello, damn bitch you still tied up?"

"Naw they just left what's up? I'm trying to chill with my girls before I leave."

"Damn, bitch, you acting like you going away and shit."

"Well, hell it feels like that, Sasha. I'm so nervous."

"Girl bye I'm bout to stop at the store grab us a bottle then I'll be over there."

"Ahh girl thanks."

"No problem be there shortly."

The dogs in the yard next door were barking uncontrollably. On a hunch, Pat snuck up to the window and peeked out of the curtain. Her eyebrows scrunched as she watched a man in black walking past her driveway. She thought back to the conversation she had with Ms. Watson. Then, immediately made sure that her alarm was set. She then called Brandy.

"Hello B Stay on the phone with me for a minute."
"Pat what's wrong? What's going on?"
"Uhm nothing just got spooked a lil. I told you what Ms. Watson said, right?"
"Yeah"
"Well the dogs were barking, it was a man outside I just…"
"Girl, say no more we're almost there anyway two more blocks and we're at yo crib".
They got out and Sasha rang the doorbell. "I bet she in there taking a sip or something," she fixed her hair in the reflection against the door.
"You already know," Brandy laughed as the door swung open.
"Hey y'all." Pat let them in.
"Man this weekend with Gerald really got you nervous huh?" said Sasha.
"Ha-ha funny. Naw for real it was somebody out there just glad I'm not alone anymore. Anyway you get the bottle?"
"Nope, we came straight here."
"No need to panic I got a bottle of Moscato in the kitchen."
Pat goes in the kitchen gets a bottle of Moscato and three glasses. "So you really think it's Ken harassing you?" asks Sasha.
"Hell, I don't want it to be but I don't want it to be some random ass guy looking to hurt me."
"Yeah I feel that. Have you called the police?"
"Naw I had mentioned it to Gerald."
"Which is the next best thing." said Brandy.
"I mean should I report it?"
"If you feel your life is in danger then yes. But if not then don't worry so much about it just be careful."
"Now have you picked out what you're wearing yet?" Asks Sasha.

"Yeah, I'm so excited in just a couple hours really I'll be chillaxing with a man."

"Don't forget fine as hell nice ass body big ole…oops my bad I'm just happy for you Pat."

Pat raised her glass, "Well, toast to a wonderful weekend."

"And to lots and lots of sex for my girl," B said jokingly.

"Cheers."

About an hour or two goes by and B looks at the clock. "Well we better be going so you can get you a cat nap. You gotta early day tomorrow."

Just as the women get up and head to the door the neighbor's dogs barked and Pat's light came on. Pat peeked out the window. There was a man dressed in all black walking past the end of her drive way. A hood was pulled over his head and a black bandana covered his face. It seemed like he was looking directly at her. Chills spread up her spine and she quickly closed the curtain and looked at Sasha and Brandy.

"This shit is getting scarier by the minute. I swear he was looking right at me."

"Pat, I don't have nothing to do. I can chill here with you tonight," Brandy said.

"Yeah so can I," said Sasha.

"Aww thanks, y'all." Pat sat down on the couch. "I would really appreciate it."

The ladies turn to each other and say, "Sleepover!"

"We haven't done this in a while."

Pat went into the hall closet and grabbed her girls some blankets for the night and a couple pillows off her bed. B grabbed the remote and flipped through the channels until she found a movie. Sasha looked in the freezer for some grub.

"Ah ha!" Pat scolded her from behind. "How did I know you were in my Cold Stone?"

"Cause you know me so well," laughed Sasha. "I'll grab the spoons," said Pat as she headed to the living room to watch movies.

Everyone grabbed a spoon and dug into the double chocolate chip. Before long all the ladies were fast asleep with the TV watching them. The alarm clock woke the three of them while the sun slowly rose outside of the house. Pat jumped to her feet to hit the snooze button on her alarm clock.

"Damn," Sasha stretched. "P, what time is it?"

"8:30a go back to sleep. I'll wake you before I leave."

All Pat could think about was what Gerald had planned for them that weekend. She couldn't wait to spoon in his arms, to smell his cologne, to kiss on his chocolate lips. It had been so long since her cookie had been bit. She clutched her legs together because the thought of him being deep inside of her made her pussy throb.

"Ooh," Pat shook her head, looking at B. "I got so many butterflies in my stomach feels like the first day of class."

"Well just don't throw up like you did on the first day of class," Brandy laughed. "Everything will be straight. Just relax and have fun. Enjoy yourself, and if nothing else have fun spending his money."

"Girl you a mess. Let me get my butt ready."

The warm water drizzled over Pat's body while she sang a sweet melody. She was imagining all the love making she and Gerald would be doing and then, there was a knock on the door.

"Pat are you almost done? I gotta pee really bad."

"Shit, bitch!" Pat shouted back. "I thought y'all asses were sleep."

"Girl, hurry up before I piss on myself."

Pat laughed, "That surely will be a sight to see."

She wrapped herself in a towel, gathered her clothes, and headed to her room to get dressed.

Brandy stood in the doorway of the bedroom and admired Pat.

"Ooh don't we look nice?'"

"Thanks, girl. I think I got everything packed let me double check."

"Pat, you can triple check and will have everything packed stop worrying."

The house phone rung and Pat quickly looked at the caller ID. It was a private number and now, her stomach was aching for a different reason. It was supposed to be a good weekend so she wasn't going to let this person get under her skin.

"Ugh," she huffed and muted the ringer.

"You're still getting those calls," asked Sasha as she walks into the room.

"Yeah off and on but I ignore them."

"What time is it?" Sasha asked again.

"9:50." said B. "What you got a hot date or something?"

"Nah," Sasha curled up her lip. "I do have a hair appointment."

"We can't check in until 11." Pat told them. "I wonder if Gerald is up,"

"He better be up all this worrying you doing," said B. "I'm bout to call him."

Before she could click on his name, the phone rang.

"Damn, I guess we're on the same page." She smiled. "Hello?" Pat answered, with a Kool aid smile on her face.

"Good morning Miss. Lady. What's good?"

"Hey, it's funny cause I was about to call you."

"I know it's crazy. I been up all night thinking about you," said Gerald.

"Aww I'm not gone lie I've been nervous, excited… uh everything I mean…"

He interrupts, "Everything is gonna be fine. We're gonna eat, drink, shop, and have a good time. You don't need to worry about anything alright?"

As she lets out a small sigh Pat said, "Alright."

"Well we can check in at 11:00a.m. I don't know when you plan on making an appearance."

"Ha." Pat threw her head back and cut her eyes at her best friends. "I'm bout to leave out in a bit so I can enjoy every minute of this weekend."

'That's what I'm talking bout now you're talking. I gotta handle a few things first then I'll meet you there."

"Ok, Gerald, see you there." She hung up.

"What he say?" asked Sasha.

"Basically he told me we were living it up this weekend on him."

"Oh hell yes!" Sasha clapped.

"Girl you deserve this go and have fun."

"I am this weekend. I'm not gone think too much. Whatever happens, happens. Right?" The three of them prepare to leave. Pat made sure she locked the house up and promised herself that she wouldn't worry too much about her stalker. It was water under the bridge and she was glad to be escaping for a while. All she wanted to do was relax and enjoy Gerald. She thought about Ken and the last time they had been together. He always had a way to make her feel like the only girl in the world until he broke her heart.

"You cool?" Brandy asked as she pulled her cell phone out of her purse.

"Yes," Pat smiled.

Brandy frowned at the phone and then, put it to her ear. "What's up, Char?"

"Auntie B, what's good? I'm on my way to your spot. I got my friend to give me a ride so I wouldn't have to catch the bus."

"Alright well just call me when your close so I can make sure I'm at the house."

"Ok Auntie bye." They hung up.

"Welp," she opened the passenger door of Sasha's car, "it's official I have a roommate. Charlene will be here in a lil while."

"Think of it as a good thing, B. You're helping her and your sister," said Pat.

"Uhm ok who's helping me?" B asked sarcastically. "I know, I know. I'm not complaining but she's getting a job. I ain't for taking care of no grown ass person."

"I hear that," said Sasha.

"Yeah let's go." Brandy got into the car.

Pat put her bags into the backseat of her car while Sasha and Brandy sped off. Then, she climbed into the car, noticing the same black car that sped off the other day. It was parked across the street from her house. She watched it for a moment but couldn't see much through the tinted windows. She was stuck there for a moment, scared to death that someone was trying to hurt her. It was time that she did something about it. She slowly climbed out of the car and started toward the end of the driveway. But before she could say anything the car sped off. Pat shook her head and got into her car. She hurriedly left the house and headed toward the hotel.

Chapter 9

It seemed like she'd been driving for hours. Damn how does an hour drive seem like forever. *Good mine is the next exit oh man there goes the butterflies again.* Pat has finally reached the hotel and pulls into the valet.

"Good morning ma'am. Here's your ticket," said the valet attendant. "Can I help you with your bags?"

"Yes, thank you. They're in the backseat."

As Pat walks into the Grand Hotel she was greeted by a hotel attendant.

"Good morning ma'am. Can I help you?"

"Yes," she shuffled in her purse for her ID. "Thank you." She looked up at him again. "I'm here to check in. I already have my room and key. I just need to be shown to it."

"Alright, I can surely help you with that. Can I see your room key?"

Pat pulls it out of her purse.

"Room 306. OK, take these elevators up to the third floor and make a right."

"Ok thank you." Pat said.

Pat and the hotel attendant head upstairs to the room. They arrive on the floor and Pat noticed her room to the left and opened the door. The attendant put her bags down.

"Is there anything else I can do for you ma'am?"

"No that's it. Thank you here you go."

"Thank you ma'am enjoy your stay."

Pat kicks her shoes off to get comfortable looks around the room and noticed a dozen of roses on the table. She instantly smiled and read the card: Just a lil something for a beautiful lady. Can't wait until I see you. She smiled while she smelled a rose. Pat pulled her phone out and called Brandy to let her know she made it.

"Hello, Pat."

"Hey ah Charlene. Yeah hold on a minute Auntie B Pat's on the phone."

B yells, "Tell her I'll call her back in a minute."

"Auntie B said she'll call you back in a minute."

"Alright Char just tell her I was just letting her know I made it."

She hung up and laid across the bed and reached for the remote.

"Let's see what's on."

Just as she starts flicking through there's a knock at the door. As she gets to the door Pat hears, "Room Service."

I didn't order anything; she opens the door.

"Good morning. Your breakfast, ma'am."

"I didn't order this."

"I'm sorry, ma'am. It was already preordered to be sent to your room along with these long stem dozen roses. Now if you would just sign here."

In awe, Pat said, "Thank you."

Closing the door Pat ran to her ringing phone, "Hello?"

"Hey Miss. lady."

"Hey you," Pat responded with the excitement in her voice.

"I should be there within the next hour then we can spend some time together."

"Alright I can't wait. I might be down at the pool when you come cause the water was calling me."

"Oh is that right? Alright then I'll find you."

"Ok."

After their call was ended Pat gets a call from Brandy.

"Hello."

"What's up girl? I was washing clothes when you called."

"Just wanted to tell you I made it that's all."

"Oh ok so how is it?"

"Girl, beautiful. He sent me breakfast and roses not to mention the ones that were already in the room when I got here."

"Girl I'm telling you this one's a keeper."

"Yeah so far so good I'm bout to change and head to the pool so if you call and don't get me that's where I'll be."

"You just enjoy yourself you deserve it. Talk to you later.

"Peace."

Pat relaxed on a water raft not even noticing the handsome rippled buff body Gerald swimming her way. Before she had the chance to open her eyes he had placed his big juicy lips upon hers. She opened her eyes and noticed the man that she had been waiting on standing right before her eyes.

"Hey." She smiled at him.

She looked at his rippled body, biting her bottom lip; thinking to herself, *damn he is fine*. "Hey sexy didn't know you looked like that underneath your clothes. When did you get here?"

"I've been here for a lil while watching you relax before I decided to come over."

"Oh ok so yo wanna swim or you wanna get outta here," asks Pat.

"It's whatever you wanna do ma," said Gerald.

"Well as much as I'm enjoying these ladies stare at my eye candy I think I'll save them the pleasure and we get outta here."

Gerald grabbed her hand, lifted her off of the raft, and carried her to the side of the pool. In the back of her mind she thought about being carried to the bed. She, then, watches Gerald pull himself out and reach to grab his towel. As she watched him rub and wipe his dripping wet muscular body she had no other choice but to go over and get some.

"Hey, you missed a spot here right on your back let me see that towel."

She began to dry his back off, patting what seemed like every inch of his back. Mesmerized by the broadness of his shoulders she began biting her lip. She visualized wrapping her arms around his waist and laying her head against his body.

Clearing her throat Pat announced, "There you're all done. I think I dried up everything." "

"You ready ma?" Gerald asked as he looked down at her freshly manicured feet "cute color".

Pat watched from the doorway of her room as Gerald walked to his separate room. Although it was a sweet gesture she wished she had the pleasure of watching him peel those wet clothes from his ass. She went into the room and closed the door. Her heart was pounding and after calming down she pulled out a sexy little black dress. She was sure that before the night was over it would end up in the corner somewhere. As Pat was finishing up there was a knock at the door. When she opened it Gerald was standing there looking scrumptious.

"You look nice," said Pat but in the back of her mind she was screaming my God this man is fine.

Gerald accepts the compliment and offers one in return, "You're looking beautiful as usual." The two just stared at each other for a while before either of them bulged.

Then the staring ended when Patricia's phone began to ring. She reached over to get her phone and noticed private across the screen.

"Somebody keeps calling me private but never said anything.

"Hum that's gotta be annoying."

"Yeah it is that's why I gotta…nothing never minds. Moving on, so what's the game plan?"

"Oh ok you leaving it up to me? Well let's go do a lil shopping or hit the movies or something."

"I guess we'll figure it out while we're gone huh?" asks Pat.

Time past by and by the time they had returned to their room it was a lil after 9 p.m. What Pat didn't know is that Gerald had arranged a lil something to set the mood right. Pat walked into her room and put her bags up and went to the next room and saw a small intimate setting in the middle of the floor. Candles on the table champagne in an ice bucket and two plates covered up.

"Oh my when did you have time to arrange this?"

"Come on now this is what I do."

Before Pat could reply Gerald's phone rings he pulls it out looks at the caller id hits ignore then puts it back in his pocket. Just as he could get his hand out of his pocket his phone rings again. He pulled his phone back out notices the same number and hits ignore this time putting it on vibrate.

"Alright lil lady you ready to eat?" he asked Pat while she put on some music.

"Ooh this is my jam."

"Dance for you" by Beyoncé was playing on the radio as Patricia rocked to the beat. Looking sexy as she danced Gerald joined her putting his arms on her waist pulling her closer as she grooved. Starting to kiss on her the kisses just started coming. He kissed her on her head then moved her hair off of her shoulder then began kissing her neck Pat licked her lips as her hormones started racing. She then turned around and was facing Gerald she stood on her tip toes and kissed his forehead his nose cheeks then his lips. Gerald swooped her up in his arms. Passion was filling the room and temptations was taking over.

Chapter 10

The two began to caress each other, feeling all over each other's body. Then Pat stepped out of her heels. Slid her dress over her head exposing the bra and panty set that she had bought with Brandy. Damn is all that Gerald could say, he unsnapped Pat's bra and began sucking her nipple. Caressing her titties in his hand as she moaned and rubbed his hand along her titties with him. He slid his hand down the front of her panties and began to play with her clit and felt that she was really wet from the foreplay. Gerald thought to his self like ahh man I gotta hurry and get up in this wet kat. He took her panties off and carried her to the bed. He laid her down began kissing her lips then worked his way down. Then finally he started kissing and sucking on the inside of her thighs. Before she knew it Pat was getting head. She swarmed and moaned as his tongue licked and poked her pussy. She raised her body up and down with every lick of his tongue. She twisted, turned, moaned and groaned grabbing the pillows to put over her face. Out of nowhere she whispered, "I need you in me" as she hinted for him to come up for air. He then wiped her juices from his mouth. Then she rolled him over and just as she grabbed his dick to climb on top he began calling her name.

"Pat! Pat."

Pat shook her head as if she was coming out of a trance, "Huh?"

"I said were you ready to watch a movie? Are you alright?"

"OMG" she muttered under her breath. "Yes I'm fine, I guess I was in a deep thought". Gerald puts on a movie and before long Pat falls asleep in his arms. He enjoys her laying on him so he doesn't wake her. He continued to watch the movie. An hour goes by and Pat woke up only to find that Gerald had covered her up with a blanket and taken off her shoes.

"Uhm how long was I asleep?" asks Pat.

"Not long but you were snoring like you was," laughed Gerald.

"OMG are you serious?"

"Naw, I'm kidding. When I saw your eyes close the second time I knew it was a rap."

'Why didn't you wake me up?"

"You looked so peaceful I knew you'd wake up eventually."

"Ooh I'm sorry babe I know this isn't the night you planned for us huh?" Pat poked her lip out. "What time is it?"

"Its 1:30 a.m. and this is exactly what I planned for just to spend quiet time with you. Alright listen here's the thing I'm feeling you I mean yeah your beautiful, independent don't rely on no nigga for shit from what I see and you got a good head on your shoulders. Now if you're asking if I wanna get down I ain't gone lie. You're different from the women I usually meet in the club or anywhere for that matter. Nowadays it's all about what you can get out of a nigga or what can he do for you. I mean I don't have a problem with buying, paying or giving out just don't try and play me for no sucka duck ass nigga you feel me? Yeah I got money, cars, own a couple clubs and shit but hey I worked hard for what I got and I just want a woman who in return who works hard for hers."

"I feel you Gerald completely understandable, ain't nothing wrong with that. I mean hey you can't sit on your ass all day and expect a fortune to come your way unless you win the lottery." Pat shrugged.

Before they knew it time had passed by it was now 3:05 a.m. and this time Gerald was the one yawning.

"I saw that Mister! Now who's the one sleepy?" Pat looked at the clock. "Ooh its after 3. I had no idea it was this late. Maybe I should tuck you in this time," laughs Pat.

"Aye I ain't complaining," Gerald made his way into his king size bed. It was more than enough room for the both of them but he kept quiet.

As Gerald got comfortable and Pat tucked him in she gave him a lil peck on the lips and said, "Thanks for a lovely day."

" Aww no problem can't wait until tomorrow."

Pat headed back to her room undressed and got in the bed.

"Ooh he is so sexy and lords knows I wanna be right next to him laying down in his arms." Pat tried to fight the urge to go get in bed with Gerald. She didn't want to seem easy but her box was lonely. "I mean I'm grown if I wanna go lay with him I can. What's the problem?" She takes a deep breath. "I'm bout to do it." Pat gets up slips on her housecoat and heads into Gerald's room. *I can't believe it's 4:30 in the morning and I'm going in this man's room. Oh well it's now or never.* She knocks on the door. For a moment there is dead silence. Pat was holding her breath, thinking that he wouldn't answer. Then, she heard the click of the lock. Gerald opened the door in only his boxers. He stepped aside and let her into the room. Then, he got back into the bed. Pat stood at the foot of the bed and slowly pulled open her robe, revealing her bra and panty set from Victoria's and pulls back the covers and slid in the bed. Pat lets out a small sigh of relief then she gets the nerve to scoot her body over and put her arm around him. Pat felt so good laying in Gerald's arms thinking to herself about how long it has been. The two then just falls asleep. By morning Gerald had gotten up taken a shower gotten dressed. Ordered room service for them before sleeping beauty had woken up. She wakes up then calls out his name, she hears nothing but smells his cologne throughout the room. She looks around and sees a tray on the table. She heads towards it and notices the handwritten note that read: Good morning sleeping beauty I didn't wanna wake you I'll be back in a bit enjoy your breakfast. "Ahh he is so sweet and thoughtful. Ooh I should've gave him some well it doesn't matter he been around this long without none. He ain't going nowhere. Let's see what we have here." Pat eats the strawberry covered pancakes eggs and bacon then rinses it down with her tall glass of orange juice. Before long Pat hears the door handle jiggle and then Gerald walks through. Pats eyes light up at the sight of him.

"Good morning, beautiful. Did you enjoy your breakfast?"

Pat replies with a smile, "As a matter of fact I did thank you very much."

"Ahh it's nothing lil lady I didn't wanna wake you so I got up went for a swim and worked out a lil bit."

"A lil bit huh?" said Pat.

"Yeah just a lil bit to keep myself in shape. Well lil lady if you excuse me I'm bout to hit the shower."

It was like an alarm went off in her head. She had made it this far and her pussy was already wet. What was stopping her from getting all of him? She quickly pulled her panties and bra off, throwing them on the bed. She stepped into the steamy hot bathroom and slipped into the shower behind him. He turned to her and wrapped his arms around her waist. Pat initiated the first move. She leaned forward and kissed Gerald on the lips then turned his head to the side and kissed his neck. He then pulled her hair back kissed her neck and pulled her closer. He cuffed her ass as their lips locked. She kissed his chest as she rubbed her hands across his chest and arms.

Gerald grabbed her titties and started to suck on her nipples. Moans and groans are the only sound being made. Gerald played with Pats clit. Pat breathes heavily as she is touched in places that haven't been touched in months. Pat returned the favor and stroked Gerald's dick. She couldn't believe how big and hard he had gotten in that matter of time. Before she knew it Gerald had picked her up and her ass was pressed against the wall. "Ooh ooh ahh ooh," is the sounds which came out of Pat's mouth.

"Damn baby you got some good pussy," Gerald moaned as each thrust got deeper and deeper.

Pat felt herself cumming as she grabbed his body tighter. Her titties bounced up and down as he raised her body up and down on his hard dick. Gerald felt himself about to cum and told Pat so that he could pull out but it was feeling so good to Pat that she didn't let him. He then came all inside of her releasing juices into her warm already wet pussy. "Baby come on let's go to the bed."

He carried her wet body to the bed. The sheets clung to them as he laid her down, kissing every inch of her body. He then opened her legs and ate her out. This was no dream this time. Pat was really feeling the pleasure of Gerald's tongue between her legs. She raised her butt up and down as his tongue twirled and poked in and around her clit. He had sucked on her pussy like no other man had. Before you knew it she had cum, and he sucked all her juices out. Gerald didn't stop he kept on licking as she grabbed his head and moved her butt in a circular motion. By this time Pat was extremely horny. She pulled Gerald up for air then exchanged places with him. He wiped her juices from his mouth sucking on the inside of her thighs then kisses her lips. Pat kissed his chest and stomach then stroked his dick. She kissed and sucked on his tip giving him pleasure. Caressing his balls in the other hand, she puts her mouth over his dick; deep throating. She gagged a couple times but sucked it like a trooper. Her head bobbed up and down slobbering on him as he pulsated. He then told Pat that he was bout to cum and tried to move her head but instead she stroked it more and caught it. Gerald laid there speechless feeling so good. Pat wiped her mouth then climbed on top of Gerald's still hard dick. As she put him inside of her she bounced up and down. Moving her body up and down she caressed her breasts leaning down to lick her nipples.

Gerald said, "Baby."

He leaned up and sucked her nipples. He flipped her over on her stomach, smacked her ass, and put it in from the back. She moaned out, "Aww ooh baby you feel so good."

Pat's body shook under his as he took a deep breath and moaned. She laid flat on the bed him on top of her. She tightened her pussy muscles around his dick and gently rocked back and forth. His thick nut filled her insides while hers soaked him. Her ass cheeks suck together with a creamy mixture of cum and sweat. Pat looked over at the clock as she caught her breath. They had finally let their desires take over and she was glad. A smile swept across her face as she stirred underneath him.

"I just wanna lay here in your arms." Pat snuggled up next to Gerald just as his phone rings.

"Ahh man just as I got comfortable." Gerald snapped his teeth. "I ain't getting up."

Just as they laid in each other's arms his phone started going off with back to back calls. "Somebody really wants you huh?" said Pat.

"Yeah you would think if I didn't answer I'm busy." Gerald looked at the caller ID. "Lil Lady let me get this."

She leans up so Gerald can get up an answer the phone.

"Yeah?" Gerald screamed into the phone. "I told you I was busy, man!"

Pat seen the change in Gerald's face from happy too angry. After a few seconds he hung up the phone and stood up from the bed. "I gotta shoot a move I'll be back as soon as I can." He told Pat.

"But baby," she whined.

"I know, and I'm sorry." He shook his head. "I'll be back before you know it." He pulled out his credit card and handed it to her. "Go get yourself something sexy."

Pat looked at him and then at the card. This nigga is really trying to put on, she thought as she reluctantly slid it from his fingers. He kissed her on the forehead and went into the bathroom.

Shit, Pat thought as she turned on the TV. She could still feel his tongue on her pussy. She wanted to make his ass stay but lying there in his sweat was close enough. She looked over at the credit card on the night stand and thought about where she was going for lunch. Pat goes into the bathroom turns on the water then hops in. Her phone starts to ring but she can't hear it due to her singing and the water running. When she finally gets out and dressed she hears the beep from a missed call. It was from her stupid ass stalker. She wished that whoever the hell it was would just leave her alone.

She puts her phone on the nightstand next to the bed and lays down. Pat is woken up by the phone ringing.

"Hello."

"Heeeey, girl I know you ain't sleep. You wait all this time to be with Gerald fine ass and yo ass sleep? GET UP!"

"What's up B? Actually Gerald left."

"What you mean he left?"'

"I don't know he got a call had to rush out and told me he'd be back as soon as he can."

"Psst what the hell that mean? He'll be back as soon as he can. Anyway what are you doing sleep at 7 p.m.? I thought you'd be out on the town enjoying yourself."

"Damn its 7 p.m.? I been sleep ever since…so what's up with you?"

"Uh uh ever since what? Don't tell me you finally got some," said Brandy.

"Ok then I won't tell you!

Brandy screamed, "OMG!!! You gotta tell me everything ooh how was it?"

"Alright calm down we started in the shower and ended in the bed and I swear that man can go for hours no lie. Shid he put my ass to sleep I laid down for a minute if you hadn't of called I probably would've still been sleep."

"DAMN!!! For real oh Gerald put it down, huh? Girl, I'm happy for you. You finally got you some."

"Ha ha yeah girl thanks! I'm really feeling him."

"I told you just have fun and don't worry didn't I tell you that?"

"Yeah you did thanks girl well let me get up and get me something to eat and I'll call you a little later."

"Alright girl enjoy!"

Pat orders her food and when it arrives a fresh bouquet of flowers comes with it. Attached is a note that read. Just a lil something to brighten your day. Pat smiled from ear to ear cause even though Gerald wasn't there she still felt his presence. "Mmm now that was good let's see what's on." As Pat flicks through the channels her phone began to ring. She smiled putting the phone to her ear, "Hello"

"What's up lil lady?"

"Nothing waiting on you to come back."

"Well wait no more I'm pulling up to valet as we speak be up in a minute."

"Okay!"

Pat jumped up, checked her hair, put on her lip gloss, and sprayed a lil perfume then lays back across the couch. The door opens Pat lifted her head up and noticed Gerald carrying bags in.

"What's up lil lady?"

"Nothing watching a movie chillin. What's up with you?"

"Ahh, I can't call it had to take care of a lil business that's all. But I do have a surprise for you. I see you ate already I guess I took too long."

"Naw Brandy had woke me up. I had taken a nap then I ordered room service."

"Well do you have room for dessert? I sure do why what you got?"

Gerald starts pulling trays out of the bag. "I got you some chocolate covered strawberries, pineapples and a can of whipped cream."

"Oh really whipped cream, huh?" said Pat.

"Yeah, you know for uhm the strawberries."

"Sure that's what you meant."

Gerald headed to the couch with the tray of fruits lifted Pats legs up sits down and put her legs across his lap. He sat the tray down on the table and massaged her feet. Pat instantly swarmed because she is very ticklish but enjoyed it. Biting her bottom lip Pat squealed, "Ooh your hands are amazing." She laid her head back then she felt his hands gliding up and down her legs to the inside of her thighs. He reached over shook the can of whipped cream, and then squirted some on the strawberries and fed them to Pat. He then kissed her lips telling her how much he missed her, how much he's thought about being inside of her. Pat kissed Gerald's forehead then his nose then his lips.

"I missed you more and I want you back in me." She whispered.

With that being said Pat lifted her shirt off and Gerald slid off her skirt. Kissing her legs moving up to her thighs. He pulled her thongs to the side and licked her clit. Moaning and moving Pat managed to say, "Ooh baby I need you in me mmm ooh aww Gerald! Ooh baby I need you."

She pulled his head trying to get him to come up for air. As good as it felt Pat knew his dick felt better. Gerald raised up and kissed Pat and said, "Come on" and heads towards the bed. He undressed and told Pat to grab the can.

"Ooh now we talking," She jumps in the bed and Gerald squirted whipped cream all over her pussy and licked it away.

Pat is totally disabled. Gerald has her legs in the air and she can't move. Pat felt her eye twitching as she began to cum the more her body shook the more Gerald sucked harder and sucked all of her juices. He came up and wiped his mouth then slid his throbbing dick into her wet pussy. Pat held onto his arms as he pushed deeper and deeper. He held her leg in the air giving her all of him as she moaned. He leaned down to kiss her on the lips and she whispered hit it from the back. Passionately he caressed her body flipping her over onto all fours. She laid there with her ass in the air. Gerald kissed and licked her clit and smacked her ass before attempting putting it in.

"Ooh wrong hole." She clutched her ass cheeks together and nearly jumped from the bed.

"My bad lil lady," Gerald tried to mask his laugh. "Relax." He whispered.

"No," she looked like she'd seen a ghost.

"Please."

Gerald put his thump in her mouth and then rubbed it against her asshole. Pat started to relax. She closed her eyes and slowly eased down in the bed. The tip of his dick pressed against her pussy. She wanted all of him. He was still rubbing her asshole but it was feeling so good as he pushed his dick into her more. He was rocking in that thing and the next thing she knew he was all the way in. This time she was gripping the sheets and biting the pillow. Gerald pulled on her hair as he fucked her like she was being punished but in a sensual way. Pat began to cum and just as she did Gerald came too it felt like an explosion. He moaned and shook as their juices intertwined. He slid out and they both just laid there.

"Damn you know how to put it on a nigga don't you?"

Out of breath Pat replies, "Whew that's you. You got me over here tripping." She caught her breath. "And to be honest I can't believe I didn't make you wear a condom! And then I almost let you put it in my ass. That's not me." She laughed.

"Baby, I can assure you. I'm clean."

"Well it would be too late if you weren't." Pat shook her head.

"I guess." Gerald pulled her closer to him and kissed her.

"I can't tell you the last time I've ever felt like this. Well I could but then I'd have to kill you."

"Oh really?".

"It just feels good to feel wanted and know that I am."

"I told you lil lady stick with me and I'll keep you smiling." Gerald leans down and kisses her on her forehead. Pat looks up at him and they just stare into each other's eyes.

Pat giggles, "Uhm you wanna hear something funny?"

"Yeah, what's up?"

"Laying here with you I mean it feels right like I can get use to this real talk."

"That's good Ma because I don't plan on letting you go."

Pat looks up again but this time they began to kiss and before long they were at it again.

As the time had passed by Pat and Gerald were exhausted. Pat laid there flicking though the channels looking for a movie to watch. She saw the reflection of her phone lighting up in the mirror. She didn't really feel like getting up but she did. It was Brandy on the phone.

"Hello"

Brandy was screaming on the phone. "Calm down, Brandy! I can't understand you." Brandy was saying that the alarm at her house was going off.

"WHAT!" Patricia's voice gets high pitched.

Just as she put her hand over her mouth Gerald sat up. "What's going on babe? What's wrong?"

Pat looks to him and said, "My door has been kicked in, we've got to go now." she tossed the phone on the bed and hopped up.

Patricia and Gerald scrambled around the room to get dressed. She couldn't believe that someone had actually tried to break into her house. They decided to go in their separate cars. Gerald called up one of his boys to meet him at Pat's house. He only knew bits of what Patricia had told him about her ex, Ken. He had the feeling that he had something to do with the break in and now was ready to kill him.

While Patricia drove she noticed a black Impala switching lanes behind her. Patricia took the next turn to head onto the freeway merging into traffic. She thought to herself, Naw it couldn't be the same car and continued to watch the road. Just as she looked into her rearview mirror she noticed the car flying up behind her. She reached for her phone and dialed Gerald to see where he was just as he answered the black car rams her from behind.

"Ahh," She screamed as she tried to keep the car under control.

"Patricia!" Gerald yelled into the phone. "Patricia!"

'Oh my God!" Pat screams. The phone flew out of her hand and on to the passenger seat. "Gerald help I'm on the freeway and this…"

Patricia's car was hit one more time sending it flipping over three times crashing into the wall. Gerald was flying trying to get on the freeway with only the thoughts of her screaming wondering what the hell had happen. Patricia's wheels were still spinning as the black car sped off. Other drivers started to pull over to help.

"911 where is the emergency?"

A frantic pedestrian answered, "We're on 96 and Ford. A woman's car was hit and flipped over and she's not moving. Please help."

"Dispatching emergency crews out now. Is the woman breathing?"

"I don't know. Her car is flipped upside down and she's not moving and there's blood coming from her head. There's men trying to get her out."

"Please tell them don't move her wait for the ambulance."

"Excuse me the operator said don't move her."

Another pedestrian yells out, "Well tell them to hurry up and send someone out here this woman needs help."

As the ambulance was coming down the oncoming ramp Gerald had started driving on the side of the freeway because of the stand still traffic due to the accident and people getting out of their cars to try to help. When Gerald finally got to the crash his heart dropped. He jumped out of his car, keys in the ignition and ran over to the crash. The police tried to keep him back because this appeared to be a hit and run. He shoved past yelling, "This is my woman."

With tears in his eyes he held her hand as the EMS workers worked to get her into the ambulance.

"Where are you taking her? Where are you taking her?"

"We're taking her to St. John just down the street but please sir you have to let go of my arm so that we can get her there."

As the EMS pulled off the lady who made the call walked up to Gerald and said, "Excuse me. My name is Mary and I called for help for your girlfriend and I told the police what I saw but I wanted to give you this." Gerald looked as she handed him a piece of paper.

"What's this?"

"This is the license plate of the car that hit her. This was no accident. They intentionally tried to run her off the road."

"Thank you, Mary, thank you."

"I hope she'll be ok I'll be praying for her."

Gerald ran back to his car and headed to the hospital. He knows no one to call. He has no numbers, he felt helpless. He calls his boy who he sent to Patricia's house.

"What up G?"

"Dog listen some mutha fucka ran Patricia off the road and old girl who saw the shit gave me the license plate number. Now are you at her crib?"

"Yeah I'm here".

"Let me holla at Brandy."

"Aye yo B here it's Gerald."

"What's up Gerald?"

"Brandy, Patricia was in a car accident she's in St John Hospital."

"OMG!!! Is she alright?"

"I don't know I'm walking in now ole girl up here said a black car ran her off the road on purpose."

"Black car? Was it an Impala?"

"Yeah how you know?"

"That car been following her sitting on her block and everything."

"Well I'm bout to get Sasha and we'll be there."

An hour and a half goes by before Brandy and Sasha make it there. They run in and see Gerald sitting there. "Gerald, what's going on? What are they saying?"

"She's in surgery. That's all they're telling me. They said they can't disclose any more information unless I was family. I almost went off on the staff. They had to call security twice, but I chilled because it wasn't doing Pat no good," Gerald explained as he put his hand over his face.

Brandy rubbed his back "She's gonna be alright. My sister is strong, she's gonna be alright." Tears fell from her eyes.

"Come on y'all. Sit down." Sasha tapped her hand on the seats next to her. "Man I can't believe this shit is happening we just spent the night at her house cause of whoever the hell this was."

"What do you mean?" Gerald frowned.

"Well her neighbor told her about somebody hanging around her house at night."

"Yeah she told me that part."

"Ok, well the day before y'all left somebody was outside her house in all black and the neighbors dogs were barking."

"I bet it was that punk ass nigga Ken ugh I hate him," said Brandy.

"Well whoever it was gone pay and gone pay hard." Gerald said with an evil look in his eyes.

Just then a nurse comes out and calls for the family with Davis. They jump up and say "Yes we're her sisters and this is her fiancé."

"Okay the doctors are finishing up and will be out in a minute to speak with you."

"Whew, ok thank you."

"No problem," said the nurse.

"I hope everything is alright. I can't imagine what's going through her head or how scared she is" Sasha sighed.

"The family with Davis" A doctor comes over to them. "I'm Dr. Nelson I worked on Ms. Davis. She was brought in from car accident which you all may know. She suffered major head trauma, lost a lot of blood, we were able to stop the internal bleeding. She has a few broken bones, but in due time I expect she will make a full recovery. She is going to need to rest and take it easy for a while and I'm also sorry to inform you that the baby didn't survive." He said, sadly.

"Baby?" The three of them stared at him.

"Yes, Ms. Davis was about six weeks pregnant. The baby hadn't fully developed and due to the blunt trauma she suffered in the accident there wouldn't have been a chance for survival. I'll have my nurse let you know when you can see her. If you have any questions my staff will be happy to assist you."

"Thank you Dr. Nelson" Gerald said as he walked away.

"OMG! I can't believe Pat was pregnant and didn't say anything. I mean," Brandy exclaimed, pausing to look at Gerald. "Did you know?"

"Naw, Ma, it wasn't mine! DAMN! Man, I gotta get outta here. I gotta handle this."

"Gerald listen I know you're hurt and angry. We are too, but Pat's gonna want to see you when she wakes up." Just as Brandy stops talking a nurse comes over with a clipboard.

"One visitor can come back."

Sasha and Brandy agreed to let Gerald go back first.

"Ok sir you have only five minutes back here with the patient and then I'm gonna have to ask you to step out."

"Ok that's fine thank you."

"Your more than welcome. Once she comes out of recovery and is moved to her room, you'll have more time to visit," said Angie.

As Gerald walks in behind her he notices Patricia bandaged like a mummy. She had bandages all around her head, her arms were bandaged, she had tubes in her nose and throat. Machines beeping all around her. She just looked so helpless, and that's how he felt. He couldn't do nothing to get her out that bed. A tear dropped. He pulled a chair close to the rail to sit next to her. "Baby I'm here. It's Gerald and I'm not going nowhere. I'm gonna make the bastards pay for doing this to you. DAMN!" he looked at the blood on the bandages. Gerald balled his fists up and began to get angry got up and kissed Patricia's forehead and left the room. Sasha noticed him coming down the hall and jumped up.

"How is she? Can we see her?" Looking at the expression on his face Sasha said, "Gerald are you alright?"

"I'm sorry Sasha I gotta go. My Lil Lady up in there fucked up I can't handle this." Tears streamed down his face as he stood there with his fist balled tight. Sasha and Brandy wrapped their arms around him as the tears continued to fall. Pat had always been the strongest of them and they had never seen her hurt. Ken was definitely the blame for all that was happening, they really couldn't see any other logical explanation. How were they going to tell Patricia that she had lost her baby though?

The nurse allowed Brandy to visit with Pat, next. As she walked into the cold room, her heart sank into her chest. Pat looked nothing like herself and who ever had done this wanted her dead. Brandy covered her mouth as she moved closer to touch Pat's hand.

"Baby girl, we're all rooting for you, you know?" Brandy said. "Lord knows I need you to come with me to the mall next weekend." She laughed. "And you should see Gerald. He's out there looking a mess. So you got to pull through this, okay?"

She wanted to start in on Pat about the baby she was carrying. Brandy was almost certain that it was Ken's child. That's probably why the old married bastard wouldn't leave her alone. It wasn't the time or the place for that, besides Pat couldn't speak for herself at the time. "I'm just so thankful that you're alright, that your alive. I don't know what I would do I if you had died" Brandy spoke softly as the tears roll down her cheeks. "You are my best friend. my sister and I don't care how long it takes I'm gone be right here helping you get through this and you know me I'm not gone just sit on this. Well baby girl I'm gone go out here and let Sasha come sit with you before that nurse come try and put us out and then you know we gone set it off up in here." As she laughs she kisses her forehead "You'll be okay, Pat."

She then walks out to the waiting room to let Sasha back just as the nurse approaches.

"I was just about to come get you."

"Well I saved you a trip now didn't I?"

"Brandy stop it." Sasha shook her head.

"I'll be out in a minute."

While Sasha's in the back, Brandy pulled out her phone to retrieve her messages, after listening she found out that her niece found a job.

"At least some good news."

Brandy goes over to the vending machine reaches in her purse to get some change.

"A dollar for a twenty-five cent bag of chips you gotta be kidding me ugh!"

Just as she opens her bag a chips Sasha comes out. " Did she come to? Did she wake up?" asks Brandy.

"No, no movement, no twitch or nothing."

"I asked that because you came back out so quick."

"Oh because they had to do a test."

"Whoever did this shit gone pay and you already know dat," Brandy bites her bottom lip.

"Ugh so what now?"

"Well the doctor said it could be awhile before she wakes up. No telling so I gave them our numbers at the desk and I wrote it on the clipboard. I told them to call us as soon as they move her to her room and absolutely NO visitors unless it's one of us. I'm not taking any chances" said Sasha.

The two hug each other as they head for the car. On the drive home Brandy's phone starts ringing and she pulls it out. "It's probably Charlene again." She mumbled as she put the phone to her ear.

"It's Gerald." He said when she answered.

"Hey Gerald. What's up?"

"I just called to say my bad for rushing up outta there like that."

"You ain't gotta apologize you good my sister knows you there for her."

"Man just looking at her laid up like that man fuck that somebody gone answer for this."

"Hell yeah," said Brandy.

"Now this Mary she said a black car right?"

"Yeah."

"Did she see who was driving? I mean like a man or lady?"

"Naw she just gave me the license plate number.

"Oh don't worry I'm gone find out who's car it was. Oh I ain't letting this shit ride. I just wanted to holla at you and tell you that. Use my number call if y'all need anything and please keep me posted about Pat."

"I sure will Gerald, alright bye."

Gerald was angry. He knew that he had to do something and that whoever had hurt Pat was going to pay for their fucking mistakes. He knew a little bit about her ex and that he had been stalking her. Seeing her hooked to all of those machines, made him sick to his stomach.

"Alright all bullshit aside, I think it was that nigga Ken," yells Brandy.

"I mean don't get me wrong I don't like him either, but wasn't he just begging for Pat to take him back? Why try and hurt her?" Sasha tried to rationalize.

"That's just it he can't have her nobody can. OMG and she was pregnant. She told me nothing happen. Ugh, I'm so mad at her." Brandy growled.

She and Pat had been friends for so long. They had never kept secrets from one another. Maybe, Pat didn't know she was pregnant. Brandy was praying it wasn't

Ken's baby, though. That would make this whole situation sicker.

"Brandy, calm down maybe she didn't want us to know, didn't want us to talk shit about her."

"Ha Ha! Your right cause you know I was gone let her ass have it," Brandy scrolled through her phone as they pulled up to Brandy's car.

"Ok, boo call when you get home." Sasha told her as she got out of the car.

"Alright, Sasha."

Brandy tossed her purse into the passenger seat as she climbed into her car. It had been one hell of a day. She sighed, turning on the radio. Suddenly, she heard a buzzing noise. She dug into the purse to find Pat's phone was ringing. It was a call from a private number. Brandy frowned and answered with an attitude.

"Hello." She repeats it again.

"Hello." No one is saying anything on the other end so Brandy hung up.

"Ugh, I see what Pat was talking about."

Before she could finish her train of thought the phone rang again. This time Brandy answers it sarcastically, "Hello." No one said anything so before Brandy hung the phone up she said, "Petty ass bitches."

Then, she put the car in drive and sped away. As she's pulling up on her block she called Sasha to let her know that she was home and to tell her someone was still playing on Pat's phone.

"I wish there was a way to trace it back to whoever it is," said Sasha.

"I know right. OMG!" Brandy shouts as she walks into her house.

"What's wrong B?"

"Somebody been in my house. I didn't leave the TV on in the Livingroom and…" She looked around.

"Oh big dummy." She laughed.

"What?" Sasha frowned.

"I forgot Charlene lives here, now. Well after a day like we've had can you blame a sista for jumping to the worse?"

"Naw you can't. Today has been stressful and I'm bout to take me a nice hot bath and I'll talk to you later, Brandy."

"Ok." She hung up.

After a good night's rest Brandy woke up to a ray of sunlight shining into her bedroom. She sat up in bed and stretched. Her mind had been on Pat all night, praying that her girl would be okay. She climbed out of bed and went to make coffee. Then, she turned on the news on the kitchen's television. She enjoyed watching the news but there was always some sad shit on. Now, with the presidential elections well underway, Brandy thought about the prospect of there being a woman president. It sounded good but it would be a small victory if the country remained in it's current situation.

She slowly sipped the hot coffee. The house phone rang.

"Hello?" Brandy answered.

"Hi, this is Nurse Catherine. May I speak to Brandy Jackson?"

"Speaking." Brandy held her chest as she waited to hear what the call was about.

"You are listed as the next of kin for Ms. Patricia Davis." Nurse Catherine said.

"Yes, she's my sister."

"Ma'am, I am calling you let you know that she is awake and asking for you."

Brandy caught her breath and let out a light chuckle. "Oh my, thank you so much for calling. I will be right there." She hung up, placing the coffee mug on the kitchen counter.

She raced to her bedroom and got dressed. As she headed to the car, she called Gerald. He was glad to hear that Pat was awake. Then, she told Sasha, who would meet her at the hospital. Her mind was going a mile a minute as she drove. She had so many questions for Pat but she didn't want to overwhelm her. The most important thing was that she was going to be okay. When she pulled up to the hospital, she turned Pat's phone back on. 20 missed calls. 10 voicemails. 5 text. Who could have called her so many times? Whoever had done this to her, wanted to know if she was dead.

Sasha was waiting for Brandy at the main entrance of the hospital. They exchanged a tight hug.

"I am so glad she's okay." Sasha said.

"Right.

Man I wanna know who in the hell did this and I bet it got something to do with those private calls. Whoever it was called earlier. I'm telling you I think its Ken or his wife. I'm telling you." Brandy confirmed as they walked into the hospital.

"Hi may I help you ladies?" A friendly nurse asked.

"Hi. Yes, you may. We're here to see Patricia Davis."

The nurse gave them a pass and directed them to her room. Patricia seemed to be asleep when they walked in. Sasha sat in the seat next to the bed while Brandy grabbed her hand. Her eyes slowly popped open and she looked around the room.

"How did I get here? Who did this to me?"

"We don't know anything baby. We're trying to figure it out ourselves," said Brandy.

"I don't remember too much. I mean I just remember being hit from the back and trying to call Gerald. Gerald. Where is he?"

"He'll be here. Calm down, don't get your pressure back up," said Sasha.

As Pat takes a deep breath, "I didn't know nothing just woke up in here this is like a nightmare. I go from a great place to a disaster and speaking of disasters how's my house?"

"It's alright Pat. Just pretty much trashed it. I didn't see what was taken if anything, but don't worry about that. Your insurance will cover all of the damages," said Brandy. "Alright, Pat, you know we love you right and wouldn't judge you right?"

"Yeah just say it B." Pat sighed.

"How come you lied to me when you told me nothing happened between you and Ken that night?"

Pat looked away. She didn't really want to talk about what happened between her and Ken. She would rather have kept it herself but the cat was out of the bag, sort of speak.

"Ugh, I don't know I was at a really bad time in my life and at the moment I gave in. I almost told you on the phone, but you were so against it when I was telling you the story that I couldn't."

"And the baby?" asks Sasha.

"Baby? What baby?"

Pat sat up in the bed, staring at her two friends. Sasha and Brandy start to look at each other and back at Patricia.

"The doctor didn't tell you?" Brandy asked.

"Tell me what?" she buzzed the nurse's station. "Can someone get in here, quick?"

Brandy held her breath. She thought they would have told her about the baby by now. It was her right to know what happened. A nurse came into the room.

"How may I help you?" she asked.

"Ma'am, is there something someone forgot to tell me?"

"Uh, what's going on?" The nurse grabbed her chart. She looked it over and said, "Oh." Then, she rushed out of the room.

"What in the hell is going on?" Pat asked. "Tell me!"

"Well, Sweetie, we don't know how to tell you this..."

Pat waited for the answer.

"The doctor said that when you were brought in, they did everything that they could but considering the trauma you sustained they weren't able to save the baby."

"Baby? What? Oh my God!" Patricia started crying hysterically as her friends held her close.

"I'm so sorry, Pat. Ooh its ok. Let it out." Brandy said as she rocks back and forth with her.

Just then in walks Gerald with a bouquet of flowers and some balloons.

"Did I come at a bad time?"

"No baby." she reached for the Kleenex to blow her nose. "You're fine come in. Brandy and Sasha was just giving me the heads up about something. Are those for me?' She reached for the flowers.

"Yes beautiful. What's up B? Hey Sasha."

"Hey, Gerald," they spoke in unison.

"Alrighty, then. B, you wanna go and grab something to eat from the cafeteria?" Sasha asked as she nudges her.

"Sure, Sasha. Alright, we'll be back up in a bit give y'all some alone time," said Brandy.

"Ok and thanks for being here," Pat smiled.

"Girl bye we're sisters."

"Hey you," Gerald touched her hand as Pat looked at Gerald tears filling the inner corner of her eyes.

"What's up Lil Lady how you feeling?"

"I'm ok and huh you still calling me beautiful after the way I look?"

"I know what you look like underneath those wraps and besides that yes I'm still calling you beautiful."

"What? Why are you staring at me like that?" asks Pat.

"I'm just so damn mad I couldn't do shit," he closed his eyes and took a deep breath.

"Baby, it wasn't your fault there was nothing you could've done to prevent this." "Patricia I should've protected you. I should've…"

Pat cut him off, "Should've what? Drove your car in the middle? Gerald I'm not blaming you so please stop it I've already loss my…"

"You already lost what?" asks Gerald.

Sniffing Pat answers, "Nothing it's nothing."

Gerald takes her hand and said, "I already know about you losing your baby and I'm so sorry."

She looks into his eyes. She just hugs him tight squeezing his neck. She lets out a huge sigh, "Baby I swear I didn't know I was pregnant I just found out myself. That's why I was crying when you walked in."

"Yeah I was here when the doctors were telling us your condition."

The ladies returned about 20 minutes later and Brandy said jokingly, "Get a room."

Gerald gets up so one of the ladies could sit down, but neither of them wanted him to get up. "Man they cafeteria food here is good as hell," said Brandy.

Sasha replied "Yeah, I gotta admit their breakfast buffet was nice."

"Hello Ms. Davis. I'm Dr. Nelson I came in a little while ago, but you were gone for testing. How are you feeling?"

"I'm a lil sore on the right side and down below," said Pat as she swarms around in the covers.

"Alright I'm going to order you some meds; get you as comfortable as possible. I want to keep you for a couple days just to keep an eye on you. Do you have any questions for me?"

"No, not at the moment. Thank you."

"Ok I'll put this order in for you and I'll check on you later. You all enjoy your visit." He left the room.

Pat gets teary eyed and puts her hands over her face.

"What's the matter Suga?" Sasha asked as they all gather around her bed.

"Yesterday was so perfect. Now, today I'm laying here in this hospital bed and I don't even know what the hell for. I'm scared to go home right now. I don't know who might be there and what's gone happen next."

"Shh," said Gerald. "I'm not gone let nobody hurt you again."

"Gerald, you can't protect me," shouts Pat.

Gerald frowned. All he wanted to do was protect her. What kind of man does she take me as? He thought. He backed away from the bed.

"Maybe I should go."

"Wait Gerald she didn't mean it like that," said Brandy.

"Gerald, she's right I'm sorry for how that came out. That's not what I meant. I mean you can't be with me 24/7 and I can't expect you to drop everything and come running when I need you."

Brandy buts in, "Well then come stay awhile with me."

"No, Brandy thank you, but you have Charlene there now and I wouldn't wanna impose."

"You know you wouldn't be imposing girl."

Gerald stands up, "Don't worry about nothing I'm gone handle everything."

He leans over kisses Pat on the forehead "I'll check up on ya later. B, Sasha, y'all take care of my girl."

Pat smacks herself, "What did I do? Damnit, he's probably not coming back and I wouldn't blame him."

"Don't beat yourself up," said Sasha.

"Did you hear what I said and how I said it? From day one he's been nothing but good to me and all things I say that to him ugh."

"Well, look if he wasn't coming back or took that shit to heart he wouldn't have told you don't worry bout nothing. Girl he got you that man ain't going nowhere," said Brandy.

"I hope not," mumbled Pat. "So what y'all got up for today?"

"Nothing much I'm chilling today no plans," said Brandy, "but truthfully I'm trying to link up with Daniel that fine ass fireman I told y'all about."

Pat smacks her lips, "Girl you a mess." They all share a laugh.

Nurse Karen comes in with some pain meds for Pat.

"Ok the doctor ordered you some meds so I'm giving you some morphine. This should kick in instantly you should actually start to feel it in a couple minutes. Now if you need anything else just press the red button on your remote. She might start to drift in and out, but she's not in any pain."

"Thanks Karen." The ladies say in unison.

"Well considering she looks spaced out, I think we can let her sleep. What you think Sash?"

"Yeah we can, Pat we're getting ready to head out."

With the no response, they knew she was out so they left and headed home.

Later on that night Brandy got a phone call from Gerald.

"Hello."

"What's up, B?"

"Hey Gerald. What's going on?"

"My bad for walking out like that, but I just needed to clear my head"

"You cool Patricia felt bad after you left, but we reassured her you were coming back."

"Thanks, but this what I called you for I wanted to know Pat sizes. I was gonna ask you to meet me over there so I could pick up a few of her things and bring them to my crib."

"Uh oh. Does this mean she's coming home to you?" Brandy said, laughing.

"Yeah, I figured I can watch out for her better with me."

"Oh ok that's what's up, and just let me know when you wanna go over there and I'll meet you there."

"Alright bet I'll holla at you later."

Charlene had been staying with Brandy for over a month. She managed to get a job and is starting to mature a lot. She was always Brandy's favorite niece. Sometimes, Brandy wished she had a child of her own but witnessing Char and her sister fight made her happy that she didn't have any. Char wasn't a bad kid she was a typical teen. So the two of them didn't bump heads often.

"Auntie B," Char sat on the edge of the bed. "Did you see Auntie Pat? How was she?"

"She was bandaged up but she's gone be alright. My girl's a trooper."

"Okay, so I am about to head to work. Do you need anything?"

"Wait how you getting there?" Brandy's eyebrow raised on her forehead.

"I got a ride and one of the girls gone bring me home." Char told her.

"Alright."

Brandy laid down to take a quick nap, which turned into the whole day. She had a missed call from the young tender she was after. She quickly dialed the number.

"Hello"

"Hey, Daniel. This Brandy. I was sleep when you called."

"What's up Brandy? And I know who you are."

Brandy starts blushing, "Oh, well just in case. I didn't want you to get us confused."

"Get who confused?"

"All the women that call you of course."

"Oh it's like that? Well honestly there's no women. I have only a few lady friends that call. I don't really have the time to go out and meet people. I mean you know my schedule be hectic."

"Oh well my bad, but how are you doing?"

"I'm good and you?"

"I'm good as well."

"What's wrong I can hear it in your voice?"

"One of my best friends was involved in a bad car accident the other day, but she's gone be ok."

"Oh I'm sorry to hear that. Can I take you out to make you feel better kind of take your mind off of it for a minute? I mean I understand if you say no, but I thought maybe you'd like to vent, or get out the house."

"Sure I would love that." Brandy smiled.

"Alright, how long would it take for you to be ready?"

"I'm getting ready as we speak. Now, are we meeting or are you picking me up?"

"I thought I'd pick you up that way we could talk more on the ride."

"Ok I'll be ready when you get here." She texted him the address.

"Ok, I'll call you once I'm close." He hung up.

"Yes I've been waiting on his fine ass to put this fire out inside of me." She spanked her ass.

Gerald hired a cleanup crew and a lock smith to get things back in order. He didn't want Patricia to see the house in pieces or to worry about it at all. He was a good man. He could have walked away when he found out that she was pregnant by another man but he stayed by her side. When he first met her, he had no clue that she would be the one. He wasn't planning on falling in love but he had and he wanted to have her all to himself. All they had to do was get passed all of this.

"He better answer this phone"

"Hello"

"Hey Gerald I was calling to see when you wanted to go by Pat's house?"

"Oh this is perfect timing, because I'm over here now I was gone call and ask you to stop by."

"Ok I'm bout to get ready and I'll meet you over there. Brandy arrives to see several men going in and out of Patricia's house. "Man she is going to be so surprised that you're doing this"

"I just want to make her as comfortable as I can at my crib. Speaking of which you wanna go by and check it out? I mean if you want."

"Sure that way I can help you set her stuff up."

"Alright, you can do that. Even though, I got people who do that."

"What!" Brandy exclaimed.

"Yeah, but just follow me." Gerald walked out of the house.

They pull up to a mansion, complete with a fountain in the driveway. He climbed out of the car and opened the door for Brandy. Pat has really found a gentleman, Brandy noted.

"Well this is my house let me show you the inside." The door is open up by Nadia the housekeeper.

"Good afternoon, Sir."

"Hello, Nadia this is a friend of Pat's. The one who I said would be staying here for a while."

"Yes I've made up the guest room for her and put fresh towels in there."

"Ok, good could you take these things to the room and show Brandy where it is?"

"Yes, right away this way. Please follow me."

"Wow Gerald is living large, got a housekeeper and guys bringing the bags in. Pat gone have it real nice when she come home."

"Here we are ma'am. This is where she'll be staying. Can I get you something; perhaps to eat or drink?"

"No, thank you Nadia."

"Ok just let me know I'll leave you now so you can look around." She closed the door. Brandy glances around the room thinking to herself like "man this room is huge". She walked over to the enclosed bathroom with the standup shower and a separate Jacuzzi tub. She lets out a huge sigh, "Calgon take me away right now." She turned the light off and went over to the king size bed covered with a parade of pillows. Just then, the men entered the room with all the bags and palettes of shoe boxes. As they brought in the last of the bags Brandy looked around and said, "Damn he really cashed her out."

Walking in and over hearing her comment, Gerald proudly said, "That's my baby. Gotta hold her down. Now the fucked up part about the whole situation gone be if she doesn't wanna come."

"Please try and stop her. This is the happiest I've seen my girl in a long time and she ain't about to pass all this up."

"Fasho," said Gerald.

"Welp let me start putting this stuff away, gotta long day ahead of us."

"Alright, well I'm gone send Nadia back in here to help you."

"Naw, she straight. I got it I'm use to putting bags of clothes away that's what we do."

"Alright then, just holla if you need something."

Brandy began hanging clothes up, putting boxes away, and filling the bathroom up with women's necessities. He went as far as getting pads and tampons, too because he wanted to make sure she had everything she needed. As time passed by, Brandy's stomach growled

"There, the last thing. I can't believe I'm done, oh my goodness. Shit. Damn, this I gotta get something to eat." She looked at her watch.

"Dang I literally been at this all day welp time to go."

As she gets to the door she spots Nadia in the hallway. "Excuse me, Nadia, could you let Gerald know that I'm finished?"

"I sure will but if you want to follow me, I'll take you to him." Brandy is admiring everything about Gerald's house. Before Nadia knocked they heard Gerald yelling through the door "I don't care how you get it but your betta gets my money."

Nadia knocks on the door and he gestures for her to come in.

"Sorry to bother you Sir, but Ms. Brandy is finished and was looking for you. I'll leave the two of you alone."

"Thanks, Nadia." Gerald said as Brandy walked in and sat down.

"Man Gerald your house is beautiful."

"Thank you thank you I try."

"Well I was just letting you know I was done and I was about to head out cause it's getting late and a sista is hungry." She rubbed her belly.

"Oh yeah that's right you haven't ate cause you've been with me all day. Let me have Nadia whip something up. Naw as a matter of fact let me treat you to dinner."

"Naw you don't have to do that. Pat's my girl I did this for her."

"I insist come on I gotta repay you some kind of way."

"Ahh alright I guess so." Brandy gave in.

"Alright B. Let me go grab my keys."

Chapter 11

"Hello."

"Good morning Sunshine! rise and shine."

"I'm up." Sasha said pulling the covers off her face.

"I'm just in such a better mood today since I'm going home."

"I bet you are," said Sasha.

"I'm supposed to be getting discharged about 11. I mean that's what the nurse said."

"Don't worry. We'll be there let me call and get Brandy up so we can get this thing cracking."

Brandy blows the horn and Sasha looks out to let her know she's coming. Sasha comes out smiling and amped up opens the door and gets in.

"What's up B?"

"Chillin ready to get our girl home."

"I know that's right she was so happy when she called me so I know she's can't wait." Sasha leaned her seat back to get comfortable and Brandy looks over at her,

"Uh uh Bitch. I know you ain't trying to go back to sleep."

"What? I was planning on resting my eyes for a minute."

"Naw, naw we're in this together wake your ass up."

"Alright I'm up." She leaned her seat back up yawning and covering her mouth. "I hope traffic clear so it's a straight shot."

"Right. Me, too." Brandy turned the radio back up.

Meanwhile back at Gerald's house he's going over everything and making sure its fit for Patricia to arrive.

"The house is fit for my baby to come home. Hope she don't be acting funny. Let me get out of here before I'm late."

Pat is geeked about going home even though she's still in pain she wants to get out of that hospital. "Ugh," she sighed. "I wonder if Gerald is still mad at me. I haven't talked to him since that day. I can't believe I'm pushing him away so fucking stupid." She rubbed her stomach.

I can't believe I was pregnant and by Ken at that. A precious baby was growing inside of me. How could I not know? I wonder if I should tell him I mean it was his. No don't get yourself sucked back in again that's how you got pregnant in the first place letting emotions take over. She heard familiar voices coming in the room and got excited

"Hey girlfriend! you ready to blow this popsicle stand?" asks Brandy.

"Heck yeah! Y'all got here quick this time."

"Yeah. No traffic during the day so we got lucky."

Pat starts lifting her head and trying to look around them at the door.

"What are you doing or should I say who are you looking for?" Brandy asked.

"I was looking to see if Gerald was coming in behind y'all, but I guess not." She was disappointed.

"Chill out sour puss he'll be here. Go back to being happy."

"It's just that after everything I've just been through I thought he would be the one person by my side, ugh." Pat sulked. "Y'all don't understand he is a good guy and I pushed him away with all this extra shit." Just

then the nurse walks in with discharge instructions for Pat and a wheelchair to take her downstairs. Pat is fighting back tears to save face in front of the girls and the nurse. Pat is in the wheelchair and ready to go they all head towards the elevators. The nurse pushes the down button and just as the doors open there stood Gerald with a dozen long stem roses.

"Aww Pat, I wanted to surprise you while you were still in the room."

She started crying "This is surprise enough for me."

Everyone exchanges hellos and Gerald hands Pat her flowers. She smelled them and noticed a card attached she pulls it out and read it out loud then got quiet.

"What's wrong?"

"Nothing this was just so thoughtful and after the way I acted towards you how could you?"

"Shh" Gerald put his finger towards her lips.

"All that's over with. I'm just glad you're better and coming home."

They all got out of the elevator and headed to the valet attendant.

"Ooh shoot, Sasha what did I do with that ticket? I know it's not upstairs I'm gone be pissed."

"Here," Sasha pulled it out of her pocket. "You left it on the tray next to the bed."

"You play too much! Dang get your life together." They laughed and she handed the ticket to the attendant. As their waiting on their cars Brandy starts talking to Gerald.

"So is everything a go on your end?"

"Yeah. I made sure her house was fixed up and got everything together at my crib so when she gets there she can just rest. I hope she goes for it"

"Where were you five minutes ago?"

"What do you mean?"

"Gerald her face lit up when she stepped on that elevator she couldn't finish reading your card. Come on now she's gone go for it trust and believe."

"Yeah, you're right I got plans for her that's my baby."

Sasha opens the door, "Alright, the cars are here."

The nurse asked Pat which car was she getting in and Gerald said, "This one. She's riding in this one."

so she pushed her over to it and Gerald helped her in.

Brandy pulls her car around and said, "So we'll hook up with y'all later right?" She winked at Gerald.

"Yeah hit us up you know where we'll be."

As Pat thought to herself, I wonder what he has in store for me? Gerald had the music playing low as they cruised. She leaned back in her seat and closed her eyes. She could really get use to all of this pampering. A smile crept onto her face.

"How you feeling baby? You good?"

"Yeah just a little uncomfortable over this bumpy road, but I'm good."

He reached over, grabbed her hand and kissed it. Then, held it in his. For the first time since the accident Pat was starting to feel secure again.

"Gerald listen," she turned to him, "I'm sorry for what I said mainly for how I said it. It wasn't that I felt you couldn't or can't protect me it was more so that at that very moment you weren't able to do so."

"Patricia now you listen I feel bad bout the whole situation. I mean I blame myself, because I shouldn't have let you go ahead, but I give you my word I'm not gone let nothing happen to you again promise that."

She looked at his face and trusted what he's telling her. Then, she leaned her seat back and tried to get comfortable.

"Yeah gone and rest Lil Lady. I'll wake you when we get there."

Gerald drove nonstop to get Patricia home quickly to let her stretch out and finally really rest. He pulled up to his house and had Nadia on standby in case Pat needed anything. He walked over to her door opened it, took off her seatbelt and scooped her up in his arms. As he's getting her out the car she woke up and asked "Where are we?"

His reply to her question was, "HOME."

He carried her inside and laid her on the bed. She looked around and thought she was high off the medication she had from the hospital.

"Is this your house?"

"Yes ma'am and I have everything you should need already here and if I don't I'll get it." He helped her take her shoes off. "I just want you to relax and let me take care of you."

He pulls the cover back and helps her get settled in bed. She looked him in his eyes, pulled his face close and kissed him on his lips and said, "Thank you."

He got up and turned the light off and closed the door. He told Nadia to check on her he had to make a run and to call him as soon as she's up.

Chapter 12

Brandy calls up Sasha after listening to her voicemail.

"Hello," Sasha answered.

"Sasha, tell me why ole boy on my voicemail talking bout he willing to give me a second chance because I know that was some bull that day on my part. I'm like get the heck off my phone."

Sasha laughed and asked, "What's up with Daniel?"

"Girl, I don't know I haven't talked back to him since the other day. He real cool but he goes days in between without calling and I don't like that."

"Why? Cause he ain't telling you how fine you are all the time all day?"

Brandy answered sarcastically, "Yes, naw but for real how am I gone get to know him if we have a long distance relationship and live in the same city?"

"Bye I can't take you serious."

"Sasha don't hang up on me I'm being for real."

"You know I wouldn't do that, but I do have to call you back my client is coming over, and I need to get ready."

Brandy smacked her lips, "Hmm well call me later. I'm bout to find me something to get into."

Just then Brandy's phone started ringing and she looks at it and shakes her head and answers, "Hello?"

"What's up Brandy?"

"Ugh nothing much Bo what's up with you?"

"Oh I can't call it trying to see if you still wanted to take me up on that offer?"

"What offer would that be?" Brandy rolled her eyes and hit the air.

"For me to take you out. I know you played me last time, but I decided to give you another chance and let you make it up to me."

Brandy took the phone off of her ear and stared at it saying to herself. "No the hell he didn't" Then replies

"Well let me see what day is good for me and I'll get back to you."

"Alright Sweetheart make sure you call me."

When they finished their conversation Brandy instantly rants on "Boy bye I ain't calling you not today tomorrow or never he got me messed up let me see what's on." The first thing that popped up on the screen was a breaking story. Unidentified man's body found in the dumpster police are investigating and looking for any clues or witnesses. If you know anything about this crime police are asking you to speak up. She thinks to herself remembering what she heard at Gerald's but brushed it off. Then she flicks through TV until she found a movie to watch.

Brandy dozed off and didn't hear her phone ringing until it started ringing again. This time she answered it, "Hello?"

"I'm sorry did I wake you?"

"Naw, you straight. What up? How you feeling?"

"I'm alright. I just popped a pill so I wouldn't be hurting. I'm waiting on Gerald to get back he left when I went to sleep said he was on his way back. I can't wait for him to come back I'm missing him already."

"And if I know him correctly the feeling is mutual."

"Well you go back to your nap you still sound sleepy."

"Alright then. I did have to get up early for a certain someone not saying any names though, but call me later if you're feeling up to it."

As Patricia hung up her phone there was a knock at the door.

"Ms. Patricia, I made you some soup I didn't know if you had your appetite back yet or not, but I wanted you to at least eat something."

"Aww that was nice of you. Thank you, Nadia."

"No problem. Can I get you anything else?"

"No, this is great thank you."

Nadia left and shut the door behind her. Pat decided to watch TV while she ate and waited on Gerald, who should've been home by now.

"I wonder what's keeping my man so long." She continued to flick through the channels to pass time by. Suddenly there is a knock at the door and she assumes it's Nadia so she shouts, "Come in."

To her surprise it was her man, "How you feeling Lil Lady?"

"I'm better now that you're home. I can't believe you went through all this trouble for me."

"I told you I got you, you need anything?"

"Naw, Nadia made me some soup not too long ago. Can you lay with me for a minute?"

"Of course you don't have to ask that just scoot over and let daddy in the bed." As they lay and cuddle watching TV Gerald's phone rings. He reaches in his pocket to get it looks at it and sends it to voicemail and then puts it on vibrate.

Pat asked, "You sure you don't want to answer that it could be important?"

"Everything that's important to me is right here in my arms."

Pat smiled from ear to ear and laid her head on his chest and closed her eyes. They watched TV until the TV started watching them and they were both asleep.

The next morning Pat woke up to a rose and a card attached, "Didn't wanna wake sleeping beauty. See you in a bit."

She gets up to go into the bathroom and while in there she hears a knock on the door. Nadia entered, "Good morning, Ms. Patricia. I made you some breakfast scrambled eggs sausages toast fresh fruit and some orange juice. I will set the tray on the nightstand for you. I'll check on you in a little bit and I'm here if you need help with anything just let me know."

"Ok thank you Nadia I will." She closed the door.

Just as she takes a bite of her toast her phone rings.

"Hello"

"Hey girl what's going on?"

"Nothing laying here eating this breakfast Nadia made me. I got my appetite back and pretty soon I'll have my strength back too."

"Well don't rush it. If I was you I'd let Gerald take care of me forever."

"Sounds good, but I still gotta work I'm just off temporarily."

"Not if you keep doing what you're doing and play your cards right."

"What am I gone do with you? You're a mess."

"I'm so serious though that man got all that house and money and no wife to share it with."

"Oh dang we're on wife now huh?"

"Girl you better get it. I'm telling you."

"I hear you, B. I hear you. Have you talked to Sasha?"

"Not today."

"I actually haven't talked to her since I've been home. I mean it's only been a couple days maybe she's been busy."

"I talked to her last night, but her client had come over so she rushed off the phone with me and that was it."

"Can I talk to you on a serious note Brandy?"

"Girl you know you can what's going on?"

"Ever since the accident, I've been having nightmares and it's really scaring me because I don't want nothing to happen to me."

"Aww, boo I am so sorry you're going through this."

"Thanks me too. I just don't feel the same no more like a part of me was taken away. Brandy, I am so scared. Oh my God. Why is somebody trying to kill me?" She broke down.

Gerald so happens to walk in, "Baby what's wrong?" He took the phone looked at it and noticed it's Brandy. He told her she'll call her back. As he held her in his arms he kept asking her what was wrong. She cried out, "Gerald, I'm so scared, and I don't know what to do because I don't know what's going on."

"Baby, I'm not gone let nothing happen to you. You don't have to be scared."

She sniffed. "I've been having nightmares since the accident I toss and turn when I do sleep and I can't shake it."

"Patricia, listen to me. I'm not gone say it's gone be easy considering all you been through but I will tell you that it will get better. I'm here for you I got you every step of the way." He lifted her chin and kissed her softly on her lips. "Alright, you cool now?"

"Yes, thank you Gerald" She sniffled leaning up to go to the bathroom to get herself together. Looking in the mirror she said "Pat get it together you can do it don't be breaking down in front of his ass already."

She pulls it together and goes back out to the room and as she's coming out of the bathroom Gerald is hanging up his phone and putting it in his pocket.

"Feeling better baby?"

"Yeah a lil bit. I'm sorry for all that. You must think I'm a drama queen."

"Not at all. I know how strong you are an all this right here showed me is that you trust me. You let me into your heart now I've seen both sides of Patricia Davis."

"How did I get so lucky?"

"No beautiful. I'm the lucky one."

Patricia yawned "oh I'm boring you is that right?" as he laughs.

"No I think it's the medication making me drowsy maybe I should lay down for a minute. Pat let's out a huge sigh "what do you have up for today?"

"Not too much gotta couple moves to shoot then taking care of my lady for the rest of the night"

"Oh ok sounds cool especially the last part" as she yawns again. He pulls the covers back slides her onto the bed and covers her up. "Yeah baby you need to rest doctor's orders"

"Only if your gonna lay with me"

"Of course beautiful." They lay peacefully until Pat dozes off Gerald gets up and leaves the room. He pulls his phone out and dials the last missed call. Yeah you've reached Sasha sorry I'm unavailable to take your call please leave a message and I'll return your call at my earliest convenience. "What's up baby I was in the middle of doing something I hope we're still on for tonight" he then hangs up. Nadia passes Gerald in the hallway over hearing his message. He tells her to look after Patricia he has to make some runs.

"Ok Sir no problem at all anything else?"

"Yeah she's feeling a lil scared just check in on her from time to time"

"Ok Sir will do" as she walks away.

"No that was all you I had no parts in that"

"Oh is that right?"

"Yes, it is"

"Man I really had a good time I enjoy being with you.

"Well your lucky cause the feeling is mutual"

"Oh I'm lucky huh?"

"Yeah you are" as Daniel kisses her on the lips. Thinking to his self "I have been waiting so long for this" Daniel pulls back an apologizes "I'm so sorry Brandy but I have been wanting to do that since I met you."

"No need to apologize your lucky cause the feeling is mutual." They began to kiss passionately Daniel grabbing her hair into a ponytail and sucking on her neck. Brandy starts moving her head in a circular motion as he kissed, sucked and continued to lick her. He took off his shirt and showed his muscular build she felt all over his chest and arms, and started kissing his neck. Moving slowly down his chest and stomach unfastening his belt. He then stood up and slipped out of his pants and boxers. He took her clothes off piece by piece carrying her into the room. He laid her down on the bed reached over in his nightstand pulled out a condom and Brandy snatched it out of his hands. "No not yet" come here as she signals for him to join her in the bed he gets in the bed and she lays him down. She began kissing and licking around on his stomach. She started stroking his dick up and down before kissing the tip and putting it in her mouth. Daniel laid there with his eyes closed moaning and playing in her hair. She was slobbering down his balls but that didn't stop her she sucked his dick and swallowed his nut. She licked his tip and crawled to the top of the bed licking her lips. He laid her down started kissing her titties and sucking on her nipples. Playing with her clit made her hornier than what she already was. He opened her legs and kissed the inside of her thighs. Then he poked his tongue in and around her pussy. He began eating Brandy's pussy sending chills through her body. She hid her face in the pillow biting every corner and she moved up and down with every lick. Her legs began to shake and shiver as Daniel sent her into pure bliss. He sucked on her wet pussy until all her juices were in his mouth. He reaches over to put the condom on his rock hard dick pulls Brandy on top of him and slides inside of her. Her juices lubricated the opening for easy access. As he holds Brandy's waist she is moving up and down riding that dick in a circular motion. She started rubbing her hands through her hair and biting her bottom lip.

He taps her thigh suggesting to roll over, Brandy gets up and bends over in the doggy style position. He slides in her again holding on to her waist she is enjoying every minute of their love making. She reaches between her legs and grabs his balls and started squeezing them in a pleasurable way. She then starts playing with her clit as he pounded her from behind. Her body began to shake as she reached her climax and Daniel stroked harder and deeper then joined her. Exhausted they both lay there out of breath, breathing heavy and sweating they both began to fan themselves. Daniel gets up to go into the bathroom and turns on the shower, grabs Brandy some clean towels so she can join him. She staggers into the bathroom and hops in, as they began to wash their bodies they play around again in the water. They cuddle a lil bit then they rinse off and get out. As their drying off Brandy notices a tattoo on Daniel's back with a name and angel wings above and reads it out loud

"RIP Ayana who's that an ex?" He looks up at her and said

"No Ayana was my daughter she was killed in a fire four years ago. The fire trucks didn't respond in time and when they did they didn't get to her in time my baby was already gone."

"I'm so sorry Daniel"

"It's alright I just realized God needed her more than I wanted her so he called her home. That's actually why I became a fireman I didn't want another parent or family going through what I went through." Brandy feeling bad about having Daniel relive his daughter's death she gets dressed in a hurry and clams up. Daniel notices the change in her attitude kisses her forehead and hugs her. "I'm fine Brandy seriously it use to hurt to talk about her but when I talk about her it keeps her alive to me." As time goes by it's starting to get late so Brandy is about to get ready to go home. Daniel tried to convince her to spend the night, but she insisted on going home.

"Naw I'd better go home maybe I'll take a rain check if the offer ever comes up again."

"Oh most definitely" he walks her to the car and kisses her goodnight. "Call me let me know you made it safely"

"Ok I will." On the way home Brandy feels bad for how the night ended even though Daniel said he was cool. "I guess I can't beat myself up considering I didn't know. Wait a minute whose car is this in my driveway?" as Brandy gets out she hears loud music coming from her house. Keys in hand she opens her door and looks around to see Charlene and some of her friends.

"Auntie B" as she turns the music down "What are you doing here?"

"I live here remember?"

"Yes I know you live here I just didn't expect you home or at least this early"

"Well I am so you and your friends need to get my house in order."

"Ok Auntie B we will everybody clean y'all mess up my Auntie don't play no games."

Brandy heads upstairs to her room pulls out her phone and calls to let Daniel know she made it safely. "Hey I was just calling to let you know I made it home"

"Good I was just thinking about you I wish you would've stayed"

"Me too now that I've had a chance to think I'm missing you already I feel like such a punk."

"Why you gotta be all that?" Daniels said laughing

"Because I just left and I'm already missing you already that's crazy."

"It's not crazy cause I'm missing you too so I guess I'm a punk too huh?"

"Naw you're a sucka" as they both start laughing. "I'm just playing I'm just playing, but for real I really like you and wanna get to know you better. I mean especially now seeing as though we already did the nasty"

"Well don't go nowhere and you will I'm all for it"

"Ok then its settled."

"Aye I forgot to ask you how is your friend doing?"

"She's good in fact I spoke to her earlier I'm surprised she didn't call while I was over there she probably sleeps or caked up with her boo. So do you work tomorrow?"

"Yeah pretty much every day this week"

"Dang so when's the next time I get to see you?"

"Soon Brandy I promise I'll make it happen for you. Now I'm the one that feels like a punk."

"Why is that?" as she chuckles

"Cause I'm committing to make damn sure I got time for you"

"Well I guess we just gone be some punks then huh? I really had a nice time tonight" "I'm glad you did, and so did I. This is the part I'm gone hate the most when we get to spending more time together."

"And what part is that Daniel?"

"The I'll call you tomorrow part."

"It's cool I know you gotta get up in the morning and you need all your rest"

"Yeah I gotta bring my A game when I'm up there on that truck I got lives depending on me"

"I commend you for that that's real shit."

"Alright Brandy I'm gone give you a call tomorrow rest well and sleep tight."

"Yes I'm bout to sleep like a baby. I wish I was cuddled up in his arms right now ugh soon B soon"

"Good morning Ms. Patricia I made you some breakfast and a tall glass of orange juice and I put your meds on the tray as well."

"Thanks Nadia I really appreciate it."

"It's my pleasure let me know if you need anything else." She left the room.

"I can't believe it's been a couple weeks already I'm so not ready to go back to work yet."

She picked up the phone to call Brandy.

"Hello?"

"What's up girl?"

"Nothing much. I was just thinking about you."

"Oh yeah about what?"

Pat really about to give all that up and go back to normal life?

"No honestly I'm not ready, but this is not my life I'm just borrowing a piece of Gerald's."

"But if could be if you wanted it to be."

"B stop it. I'm going home and that's final, and you're still coming to help me pack right?"

"Yeah I'm still coming let me get up get something in my stomach and I'll be there."

"Ok thanks. You're the best."

"B crazy but that's my girl and speaking of girl I haven't been talking to Sasha. Let me call her. I can't believe I got her voicemail. Hey girl it's me I haven't seen you in a minute I miss you. Hey look Brandy coming over to Gerald's to help me pack you should come and not just to help but so we can catch up. If not, I'll be home tomorrow"

Pat got up to start packing she goes to the door to see if she saw Nadia to get some bags from her. She looks down the hallway both ways so she decides to walk around and see if she can find her. She seen a light on under the door and knocks before she entered. She called out to Nadia to see if she was in the room. She looked around and it was empty so she turned to walk out but as she walked out Gerald was walking in.

"What are you doing in here?"

"Oh Gerald. You scared me. I'm sorry, I was looking for Nadia; seen the light on and thought she was in here."

"I didn't mean to scare you. What are you doing out of bed?"

"Baby, you know I'm well enough to walk. I was going to start packing before B got here. That's why I was looking for Nadia"

"I wish you would reconsider my offer and stay a lil while longer."

"Aww, Gerald it sounds good but I need to get back to my life, my job and my house ugh my house."

"See that's what I'm talking about. You're not ready to go back to your house."

"That might be but I can't stay here forever."

"You could if you wanted to."

"Shut up, Gerald." She snapped her teeth.

"Pat, I'm so serious having you here these past couple weeks made me get used to having you and seeing you whenever I wanted to."

"Gerald, you have that already all you gotta do is say the word and I'm back here or you at my place."

"But it's not the same."

"Aww you gone miss me, Daddy?" She put her arms around his waist.

He looked down at her and said, "You already know." He kissed her forehead.

"Well I should go ahead and get started because it seems as though my wardrobe has gotten tremendously larger since staying with you."

About an hour later Brandy arrives at the house walks in and gives Patricia a hug. "I see you started without me didn't think I was gone show, huh?"

"Naw, I wanted to get some of the stuff out the way before you got here. I called Sasha last night and told her to come over and help me pack but I got her voicemail."

"Yeah she has been a lil distant lately, but I don't know" Brandy shrugged her shoulders.

"Gerald doesn't want me to leave."

"Shit, girl I don't either I like getting waited on all the time and don't gotta pay for it or leave a tip."

"You so silly."

"Pat, I'm so serious like for real. Where else you gonna find a deal like this real talk?"

"I know but..." She sighed.

"But what Pat? This is your chance so take it you only get one chance to live."

"You really think so?"

"Hell yeah. I think so two times"

"What about my job?"

"Pat you run your own office you can do it from here."

"Brandy, listen this is my life we're talking about you really think so? And I'm not moving too fast?"

"Patricia, you're like my sister. I wouldn't steer you the wrong way. This is the happiest I've seen you in so long and I'm absolutely happy for you."

"Thank you girl." The two hug.

Pat wiped the tears from her eyes and said, "Ok maybe I'll give it a chance."

"Yes." Brandy slapped her five.

"Girl I didn't really wanna give all of this up either. Alright let me go tell him."

She went in the hallway and coincidently, Nadia was there.

"Nadia could you get Gerald for me please?"

"Yes, Ms. Patricia and if you don't mind me saying I'm glad you're staying."

"How did you know?" Pat looked at her.

"I just knew." She winked her eye at Pat.

She goes to get Gerald as Pat headed back to the room. With a weird look on her face Brandy asked, "What's wrong girl?"

"Nadia knew I was staying but how?"

"Even she knew you couldn't resist all of this and that you would be a damn fool." Brandy said, sarcastically as Gerald walked in.

Pat turned to him. "Is the offer to stay still on the table?"

"Hell yeah, hell yeah," he said, with excitement.

He picked her up and spun her around. "Aww you guys are so cute."

"Baby you just made me so happy you just don't even know it. Alright let me see first we gotta get a truck, we gotta get boxes, gotta get my crew together"

"Gerald..." Pat interrupted. "Slow down first we gotta figure out everything. Now are you sure your cool with this because I don't wanna invade on your personal space as a bachelor."

"Come on now baby. I been asked you to come chill with me quit playing."

"Yeah you did."

"Alright, then. So stop packing get up and let me take y'all out to celebrate."

"Aww you don't have to do that," Brandy nudges her.

"Shh girl the man said he wanted to take us out to celebrate grab your purse."

"Ok I'm in let's go." Pat smiled.

"Thank you again."

"No problem, Lil Lady anything you want."

"Be careful. I might just take you up on that offer."

Just as they were leaving out Gerald's phone rings and he hits ignore.

"You sure you don't want to get that?"

"Yeah I'm sure it's nothing it can wait."

"Ok, good cause tonight you all mines."

"I thought the doctor said wait until after your checkup."

Pat hit him on his arm. "Not that silly. I meant no phones just us caking."

"I know baby you got me. Come on let's go."

"Well, thank you Gerald for a wonderful evening and I guess I'll see y'all love birds later. Call me tomorrow, Pat."

"Alright."

When they got home, Patricia started toward the guest bedroom. That had been her home for the last few weeks. It was a cozy little place that kept her mind off of everything that was going on.

"What are you doing Lil Lady? That room is for guests only" he said, sarcastically. "Occupants stay in the room down the hall."

Pat looked over at him, smiled and shook her head, "Now this way baby."

He opened the door. Pat's eyes lit up there were candles around the room, rose petals thrown across the bed and floor and a big white stuffed bear sitting on the pillow with a box attached. "OMG!" Tears were falling from her eyes.

"When did you have time to do all of this?"

"Oh I have my ways. Check out the box."

Just as Pat went to open the box she started hearing Luther Vandross coming from out of nowhere. Gerald had turned on the radio and was down on one knee. As Pat open the box she turned around to see Gerald kneeling down. She gasped and covered her mouth with her hands and started crying. "Baby since I met you, you've changed my life and I don't wanna be without you. Patricia Michelle Davis will you do me the honor of becoming my wife?"

With a shocked look on her face, she pulled him up and screamed "Yes!" She started kissing him passionately. "I can't believe this. OMG! I can't stop crying I'm so excited. Baby I love you I love you so much."

Chapter 13

Pat returns to work and on her first day back it is full of surprises.

"Ms. Davis these flowers just came for you."

"Aww they're beautiful must be from Gerald. He has such great taste."

"Again it's good to have you back Ms. Davis."

"Thanks it's good to be back. Let me read this card."

"Just wanted to wish you a good first day back. Enjoy your day Lil Lady."

"Aww, I miss him already."

Her phone rung and by the caller id it's Sasha.

"Well, hello stranger. What's going on?"

"Nothing I just wanted to apologize for not coming through the other day. I've been extremely busy."

"It's cool girl."

"Naw you my girl and I should've been there."

"Well, you're here now and I'm glad I got you on the phone hold on let me call Brandy."

"Hello"

"What's up B?"

"Nothing much. Chillin what's up?"

"Well while I have both of y'all on the phone," Pat started.

"Wait who else on the phone?" asks Brandy.

"Sasha is," they exchange hellos.

"Ok. Ok. I wanted to tell you both at the same time. I'm so excited last night Gerald proposed to me and I said yes."

"Of course you did. OMG! I'm so happy for y'all," said Brandy with excitement.

"Yes congratulations." said Sasha.

"Well, I don't mean rain on your parade but I have to call a client really quick before it gets too late."

"Ok girl call us later."

What was that all about? Pat wondered but didn't give it a second thought.

"I don't know but back to you girl I knew it I knew was just a matter of time. I said if you played your cards right all that would be yours didn't I?"

"I gotta admit you did. Wow I still can't believe it myself it's all happening so fast."

"Girl enjoy it. Don't let life pass you by. So when are you inviting me over for tea?"

"Oh so you got jokes huh?"

"You know I'm just teasing but I'm so happy for you girl you deserve it. I'm gone let you go though so I can track down my man so I can get to where you at."

"Ok girl. I'll talk to you later"

Chapter 14

Sasha was heated. She couldn't believe the bullshit Patricia had just told her. She quickly dialed up his number.

"Yeah so I had to be hit in the face with y'all lil announcement huh?" She asked.

"Oh yeah. I've been meaning to tell you. I just haven't gotten around to it." Gerald lied.

"Oh really? You haven't gotten around to it. Yeah ok. That's real though. I couldn't even get a heads up. That's some bullshit!" She shouted.

She was infuriated. There she was, trying to get a piece of the pie but this nigga was out getting engaged and shit! Oh hell no!

"Sasha, I mean what? You knew what it was from jump before we even got down so stop fronting." Gerald snarled.

"Now I'm fronting?" She snapped.

"Yeah you fronting."

"Naw I ain't fronting. Fronting is making our lil announcement to everybody."

"What announcement we got?" Gerald looked down at the phone.

"Oh nothing much, daddy!"

"What! Man, hell naw. You tripping. Get outta here. Yo ass ain't pregnant."

"We'll see in a couple months. Now, I hope this fits into your lil fairytale life y'all living."

"Naw, Sasha you the one living in a fairytale life if you think you're having my baby."

"Is that a threat?"

"Take it how you wanna take it but don't take it lightly."

"Whatever nigga!" she hung up the phone.

"DAMN!" Gerald's nostrils flared up. "Man I gotta handle this shit."

Beep. Beep

"Yes Nicole?"

"Ms. Davis is there anything else you need me to do before I go?"

"No, nothing that I can think of."

"Ok well. I'll see you tomorrow."

"Ok Nicole see you tomorrow."

About ten minutes goes by and someone knocks on the door.

"Nicole could you get that on your way out? Nicole?" as she calls out.

"Oh she must be gone. Well maybe that's Nicole and she forgot something."

Pat opened the door to find an envelope on the ground with her name on it in big bold letters. She picked the envelope up and looks both ways up and down the street as to see who dropped it off. She pulled out pictures of her from her house and a pair of her panties. She instantly pulls out her phone in a panic and called Gerald.

"What's up, baby?"

"Gerald I need you right now. Somebody sent an envelope to my job with pictures and a pair of my panties talking bout they got to me once it's not hard to do again."

"Wait, calm down baby I'm in the car. Lock your door. I'm on my way."

"Ok baby. Please hurry."

Gerald called up Doug.

"What's up G?"

"Yo meet me at Pat's job asap."

"I'm on it. What's going on?"

"I'll fill you in when you get there."

"Alright bet."

"These mutha fuckas wanna keep fucking with the wrong one when I find out who this bastard is he's a dead man."

Pat was startled by her phone ringing. "Hello?"

"Dang girl. What's wrong with you?"

"Ahh B it's you! Somebody trying to scare the shit out of me."

"Why? What's going on?"

"Somebody left an envelope outside the door here and it had pictures and a pair of my panties in it and it had to be the same person that broke in my house ugh."

"Just relax girl don't get all worked up and back in the hospital. Breathe. Did you call Gerald?"

"Yeah, he's on his way."

"Ok I'll stay on the phone with you until he gets there."

"I can't believe this shit now I'm glad I'm moving in with him. Hold on B this him calling now." She clicked over. "Hello?"

"Open the door bae. We outside."

The phone clicks back over to Brandy, "What he say?"

"They're outside. I'm opening the door now."

She saw Gerald and ran straight into his arms as his boys stand guard. "Are you alright?"

"Yes but I'm scared as hell because this is never going to stop until they kill me," She burst into tears.

"Aww Pat don't cry Pat Pat." as Brandy tried to get her attention through the phone. "Baby I'm not gone let nobody hurt you let alone kill you I promise." she grabbed some Kleenex off of Nicole's desk and wipes her face. Realizing Brandy was still on hold. "I'm sorry girl."

"You good boo. I'm just glad he's there to comfort you and reassure you that you're gone be alright. Well, gone head with him I'll come by later and check up on you."

"Ok thanks, can you take me home Gerald?"

"Of course Lil Lady. Where are your keys? I'm gone have Doug bring your car home." He tossed the keys to Doug. He opened the door for Pat "Let's go baby." they headed home. The whole ride home Pat was real quiet and more afraid than ever. As they pull up she gets teary eyed but hides her face. Doug parks Pat's car in the garage and hands the keys to Gerald. "Naw keep them I want you and the boys to stake out Pat's house go in turn on some lights and make it seem like she's there."

"Alright G I'm on it we gone catch this son of a bitch TONGHT!." Gerald goes into the house to find Patricia crying with her face buried in the pillow.

"Patricia I'm giving you my word and I need you to trust me do you trust me?"

"Yes, I trust you but..."

"No but's. Now come here. Let daddy hold you." She sighed.

"I feel so safe with you I just wanna feel like this when I'm not with you"

"You will. Pat you will."

Chapter 15

Brandy's phone rung and she answers it so sexy like, "Hello?"

"Hey Brandy what's up?"

"Oh nothing much. I was just thinking about you."

"Oh were you? I guess it's true then, huh?" Daniel quizzed.

"Guess what's true Daniel?" Brandy's eyes widened.

"That we're both punks." Brandy bursts out laughing.

"I guess so because I've been wanting to see you since the last time."

"Well wait no more open your door."

Brandy dropped her phone and ran to the door she looked outside, both ways with a huge grin on her face. She stood there looking, then closed the door and ran back to her phone. She can hear Daniel laughing.

"Oh that was funny, huh?" Brandy snapped her teeth.

"I'm sorry baby. I couldn't resist. I'm sorry." he is cracking up.

"Oh it's that funny huh? Your gonna pay for that I thought you were here. That was mean."

"Aww Brandy is your lips poked out?"

"Yes as a matter of fact, they are," she said, sadly.

"You want me to kiss them?"

"Yes I do, but you can't."

"Yes. I can open the door." Daniel smirked.

"Oh hell naw I ain't falling for that shit again." She rolled her eyes.

"Come on Brandy. Open the door."

Brandy looked out the window and there was Daniel standing with flowers in his hand. "Aww you a punk. You play too much. What are you doing here?"

"Oh well I can leave" He turns to walk off the porch.

Brandy snatched the door open.

"Get your butt over here and kiss me" She reached for the flowers.

"Yeah I got one of my homies to cover my shift tonight just so I could see you sooner." She puts her hands on his cheeks and kisses his lips, "You are so sweet."

"I'm sorry for just popping up over here like this I don't want you to think I'm a stalker or nothing."

"I know you're not a stalker a punk maybe, but not a stalker."

"Oh you full of jokes huh?"

"Yeah just a lil bit now let me go put these in some water and I'll be right back." She leaned over to kiss him. Just then Charlene walks in the house and is caught off guard by a man sitting on the couch.

"Oh Uhm hello…" She spoke.

"Hi how are you?"

"I'm fine you must be a friend of my aunts. I'm Charlene, but everyone calls me Char."

"Well nice to meet you. I'm Daniel and your aunt is in the kitchen."

"Ok, thanks." Char smiled and switched away.

"Oh hey Char. Did you meet you Daniel?"

"Yes he's cute and seems nice like a gentleman."

"Yeah, he is isn't he?"

"Well don't spend all your time in here while he's out there. I'm going to my room."

"Girl I use to change your diapers now look at you all grown up."

"I'm just saying"

They both share a laugh as they walk out of the kitchen.

"Nice meeting you, Daniel"

"It was nice meeting you too Charlene I mean Char."

"So Daniel I've been wondering something ever since you walked through my door"

"oh yeah and what's that?"

"Are you as horny as I am?"

"Man, I've been horny since you said hello."

She led him by the hand to her bedroom. She threw the pillows and ripped the sheets back. She took off her clothes as Daniel took off his. She hopped on the bed kneeling over so that he could play with her clit. He leaned forward and put his face between her legs licking her from behind. She reaches for one of the pillows left on her bed she grabs that pillow and lays forward on it burying her face in it silencing her moans. As she rocked back and forth she lifted her head and whispered "put it in." He slid his rock hard dick into her warm and wet pussy making her moan instantly. He grabbed her waist as he slid in and out stroking harder and harder with every thrust until he moaned out "ooh baby I'm bout to cum all in this pussy" he kept going until Brandy gripped the sheets and squeezed her pillow tighter. Her leg began to shake as he fucked harder and faster then she moaned out as she came herself. Daniel began to slow down knowing from the juices making her wetter that she had just came. He slides out and they lay there. Brandy lays her head on his chest.

"I'm so happy I found you."

"Are you?" asks Daniel.

"Yes I've dated a bunch of bums that actually weren't worth my time. I didn't really see myself with them long term wise. They just satisfied me for the moment I guess."

"Yeah that's how I been feeling. I mean after my daughter died, me and her mom argued all the time. We blamed each other and eventually went our separate ways. I never really stayed in a committed relationship too long, because I didn't really allow myself to love again. With you it seems right it seems easy."

He held her tighter and she snugged closer to him.

"Well see we were made for each other." She leans up and starts kissing him then he pulls her body on top of his and she straddles him. Starts kissing his neck he rubs his dick against her still warm pussy and gets her wet. She slides down on him and they make passionate love.

Rolling around all over the bed messing up the sheets once they were finished this time they hit the showers. Washing each other's bodies holding each other tight enjoying the moment they were in.

"So it's getting late huh?"

"Is that your way of asking if I want you to stay?"

"Too subtle huh?"

"No not at all, and I would love for you to stay."

They climb in bed and lay in each other's arms before long Brandy falls asleep and Daniel just watches her and kisses her forehead. Thinking to his self "man I really like this woman I hope this works out I can see myself with her in my life long term." He closes his eyes and falls fast to sleep.

Chapter 16

"Hey bae I just wanted to thank you for taking such good care of me and loving me the way you do. I can't wait to be Mrs. Gerald Briggs. See you later. I love you." Pat left a message on Gerald's phone.

There is a knock at the door and Pat goes to open it and to her surprise it was Brandy. "Hey girl. Why you ain't' call me? I didn't even know you were coming over

"Because I wanted to surprise you and see that look on your face that you got right now."

"Wait a minute speaking of looks you got a glow. What's really going on?" Pat got excited.

"Nothing much except me and Daniel have been seeing each other about every chance we get."

"That's great Brandy. I'm so happy for you."

"Me too. Girl, with all the losers I've been with."

"Maybe we'll have a double wedding," said Pat.

"I wouldn't say all that, but who knows."

"Have you heard from Sasha?"

"Yeah I talked to her the other day she said she was gone call you and stop by."

"Oh well I haven't heard from or talked to her since we got engaged." Pat toyed with her ring. "Like she's trying to avoid me and that's not like her."

"Damn right as of matter of fact let's ride over there."

"Alright let's go." As they drive and approach Sasha's house they notice Gerald's car in the driveway.

Pat's heart sank into her stomach. She and Sasha had been tight for so long that she knew all of her secrets. She remembered a time that she slept with her sister's man. If she would do it to her blood, what would stop her from sleeping with Gerald. Her instincts were to hop out the car and go crazy on their asses.

"Wait," Brandy grabbed her by the arm. "Don't go in there all crazy."

"Nah, fuck that." Pat spat. "Let me go."

"It's probably nothing."

"Is she the bitch that been blowing up his phone?"

"The hell are you talking about," Brandy frowned.

"Look, I heard some chick yelling at him on his voicemail. Don't know what she was saying but he was pissed." Pat reached for the door. "I swear..." she hopped out and crossed the street.

As they approached the house, they could hear Sasha yelling.

"No! I don't want your fucking money. She's going to find out today."

Pat shook her head and tried to make sure she was hearing correctly.

"You are not having this fucking baby." Gerald shouted as the front door swung open.

Sasha and Gerald looked like two deer caught in headlights. He stepped toward Patricia and she stepped back, shaking her head.

"What the hell are y'all doing?"

"Look I can explain," Gerald offered.

"What? Explain that..." She pointed at Sasha's protruding belly.

Gerald's face went sour. He had been caught red handed. How could she had been so stupid? There she was letting her guard down for a man who didn't give a shit about her. She looked at him, and then at her best friend. This was a woman who she had gone to bat for, one that she would have spent time in jail for but she did this.

"We...well...Pat...I didn't mean for this to happen." Gerald touched her arm but she snatched away.

"So what? Did your dick accidently slip into her pussy? Tell me? What didn't you mean to happen?" Her eyes burned a hole in his chest. "And you," she turned sharply on her heels, "You were supposed to be my girl, my friend. How could you? You know what," she threw her hands up, "y'all can have each other."

She turned for the door. Gerald raced after her, calling her name. Brandy and Sasha stood in the middle of the living room, staring at one another.

"You dead wrong for this!" Brandy gawked at her. "If you weren't pregnant, I would beat yo ass." Brandy stormed out of the house.

Brandy hopped in the car and sped off while Gerald was still begging. Patricia was crying hysterically. Her face was turning red.

"Pull over." She said. "Please."

She opened the door and threw up.

Pat gets back in wiping her mouth and crying. "This is some bullshit. I can't believe this. What did I do to deserve this? I mean I'm not perfect, but did I really deserve this?"

"No, sweetie you didn't deserve this." She rubbed her back. Brandy turns the radio on to break the silence so Pat could just be to herself right now.

"I don't know what to say or do to make this better so I'm just gone be quiet and drive." Patricia set in the passenger side and cried the whole drive home.

"Are you sure this is the right place to be right now?"

"Yes, I need to get my shit. Come on help me please before he comes."

"Alright, I'm behind you. let's go."

Nadia answers the door, noticing her crying. "Hello Ms. Patricia. Is everything alright?"

"Everything is fine Nadia. Could you get us a couple of big bags please?"

"Yes right away. I'll bring them to your room."

Pat starts grabbing all her clothes out of the drawers and hanging in the closet. "I can't believe this mutha fucka had me laying up in his bed, waiting on him every night while he was in her bed… making love to me thinking about her." She snatched her shirt off the hanger. "All these months I've waited thinking he was too good to be true. How I was so lucky to have him, and all this time he was playing me like I was stupid. How could I have been so blind? Brandy how?"

"He had us all fooled not just you."

"And lil miss innocent huh? I can't believe out of anybody in the world. I would've never in my lifetime suspected Sasha to come at me like this. That's my dog you don't understand," she breaks down.

Brandy held her and tried to comfort her. "It's gone be okay baby girl. I'm gone help you through this I promise."

Just then Brandy's phone starts ringing and she answers. "Hello?"

"Hello, beautiful just calling to see how your day was going?"

"Hey Daniel not to cut you off but I'm over here with Patricia. Shit just went down. I'll call you when I leave ok?"

"Ok."

Brandy continued packing Patricia's clothes in the bags then headed to put them in the car. She comes back in to find Patricia had climbed up in the bed and was crying her heart out. "Come on Pat so we can be gone before he gets here, because I know you don't want to bump into him right now." As she pulls herself to get up she slides her ring off of her finger and puts it on the dresser.

"Let's go cause the last thing I need is to run into his lying ass trying to plead his way out of this."

As they pulled off Gerald pulled in ran in the house and went straight to the room where he saw the empty hangers swinging in the closet. Drawers emptied out and he glances over at the dresser and notices her ring he gave her. He picked the ring up and held it tight in his fist. "What the fuck man? I gotta handle this. Patricia ain't going nowhere" slammed his fists on the dresser.

On the drive home, Sasha tried calling Brandy's phone and she shot her to voicemail. "I don't know why she's calling me. I ain't got shit to say to her trifling ass. Since when do we backstab each other?"

"I mean I knew it was something. I just couldn't put my finger on it."

As they pull up to Patricia's house they both get out of their cars.

"I'm so glad I kept my house for a rainy occasion like this."

They start unloading the cars.

"You can go ahead leave the bags right there, because I know Daniel is waiting on you to call."

"Naw I told him I was with you. It's cool."

"See you're a real friend Brandy and I'm so glad you're here for me, but go get your man I'll be alright. I'm just gone take a hot bath and lay down."

"Are you sure? Cause you know I'll spend the night."

"Yes, I'm sure one of us needs to be happy."

"Ok I'll call you later to check on you and remember I'm here for you, you're not alone." She hugged her goodbye.

"What a day I'm having I love my man and my best friend at the same damn time I was not prepared for this shit." She cried.

After she had her bath, she laid down and fell asleep for a couple hours and was awaken to Gerald blowing her phone up.

"I'm not answering none of his calls. I hate him for putting me in through this. Just leave me alone and go over your baby mama's house and bug the hell out of her."

After being sent to voicemail several times he sends her a text saying "Baby please call me."

"Shid I wish the hell I would call you back, ugh. Lord please help me get through this." She laid back down to sleep.

The sun was shining and the dogs were barking that meant it was morning and a new day. Patricia heard a knocking at her door so she gets up to see who it is. She looks through the peephole and notices a delivery truck in front of her house. She opened the door, "Can I help you?"

"I have a delivery for a Patricia Davis."

"You can send whatever it is back I don't want none of it."

"Uhm ma'am are you sure? It's already paid for."

"Yes, I'm sure. You have a nice day." She closed her door. "The nerve of him think he can just win me back by sending me flowers or whatever I'm so good on him. It doesn't make no sense. I feel so lost this was not supposed to happen to me to us. Yesterday I was in pure bliss and now I'm in pure hell."

Pat couldn't believe Sasha was pregnant and by Gerald. Oh my God we were supposed to have a baby not them. How can she ever look Sasha in the face after she betrayed her like this? She betrayed their friendship, and their trust. Patricia should've just kicked her ass, baby or not. Cause that bitch wasn't thinking about her laying up after losing her baby, why should she care about her's? She was interrupted by her phone ringing, "Hello?"

"Hey girl. How you feeling?"

"Miserable soaking up in this depression. I never knew I could hurt this bad. It's like my heart has been ripped out of my chest repeatedly."

"It's gone hurt Pat cause it's fresh and I'm not lie. It's gone take time to get over all of this. I'm just sorry you're going through this. I mean he got you over," she paused.

"Ken? Gone head and say it Brandy you can say his name I'm not going to break."

"Yeah he got you over Ken sorry ass and he turned right around and did this."

"I'm more hurt by the fact when I got out the hospital they both were all concerned for me and hurt all the while they were fucking each other behind my back. I can't believe that bitch is pregnant, I just wanted to slap that baby out of her stomach. And his ass keeps calling and even had the nerve to send me flowers and shit this morning boy bye I sent that shit back."

"Well do you feel up to some company? I don't have any plans until later."

"Sure, why not? I have nothing else to do."

"Ok. Well I'll be there in a lil bit to scoop you up."

As she was ending her call with Brandy her phone started ringing in the process and to no surprise it was Gerald. Her gut knew not to answer it but her heart wanted to hear him beg and plead for her to take him back.

"Baby please don't hang up just give me five minutes. I love you so much. I understand the hurt I caused you I should've been man enough to admit what happen. I don't expect you to forgive or forget overnight. I know it's gone take time. I just want you to know when you're ready to forgive me to give us a second chance I'm gone be here waiting I love you." Then, he hung up. A tear falls from her eye as she still holds the phone to her ear listening for one more word.

"Pat don't fall for that. Please don't give in. That son of a bitch is having a baby by your best friend. I can't do this how do I go on from here? I feel so fuckin stupid all this time I'm sharing about how in love I was I gave her the invitation."

She hears a horn honking outside she gets up to look out the window to see that it's Brandy getting out of the car.

Patricia runs to the bathroom to try and get herself together before she opens the door. She opens the door after Brandy knocks and said, "my bad girl I was in the bathroom"

"Hmm"

"What? I was"

"Yeah you probably were but I can see it all in your face you were in here crying." As Pat rubs her eyes

"Man this is harder than the first time I mean this time the stakes is higher the ante is up."

"Pat listen I'm here for you whether you wanna scream and pull your hair out. Lay on my shoulder and cry all night or just need to vent and want me to listen."

"I know girl thank you"

"Now let's get you out this house and get some fresh air it'll do you good." They head out the door and out of the blue Patricia's phone starts ringing and private is displayed across the caller id. "I guess they ain't got nothing else to do besides play on my phone. I wouldn't put it past either of them that they were the one's all this time calling private."

"Hold on Pat." Brandy put her finger up as she answered the phone. Daniel's calling. "Hello"

"Hey baby, just calling to make sure we were still on for tonight and to see if you were missing me yet?"

"Of course I am. You already know"

"Brandy, you're such a punk." Daniel bursts out laughing.

"Yes I am and my heart is still open."

"You so silly. Ok, well I'll see you tonight."

"Alright where were we?" She looked as Pat stared at her. "What?"

"You are glowing. That's that same glow I had whenever Gerald called me."

"Whatever girl. You're bugging."

"Just admit it girl. You're in love." Brandy stares out the window sitting at the light.

"Yeah I am and he is so amazing he really completes me. I think he feels the same way about me I hope I'm right and not moving too fast." She cracked a smile.

"That's good. I'm happy for y'all. I can't wait to meet this guy. Finally meet the guy that got my sister gone and head over heels."

"I can't take you serious. Pat you a mess." They share a laugh.

Pat was happy for her friend but she couldn't help but to be reminded of the love she once had for Gerald. Honestly, the love was still there. It was fucked up that Sasha would sleep with him. Her best friend was having a baby with her man. Had they been doing this all along? Were they the ones stalking her? Damn, her head was all messed up. She closed her eyes while she and Brandy drove around aimlessly. She was humming the song on the radio when Brandy tapped her on the shoulder.

"Girl…" Brandy shouted. "I know yo ass ain't sleep."

"Nah. I'm just happy to be out of that damn house." Pat laughed.

"I know that's right." Brandy popped her lips. "So, look we bout to shoot to the mall. I need to grab a couple of things. You don't mind?"

"Nah. What's up with Char?"

Brandy rolled her eyes at the question. Although Char was her baby girl, she was starting to see what her sister was talking about. When Daniel was around, Char had an extra pep in her step, wearing little shorts and shit. At first, Brandy didn't think anything of it until Char said something to Daniel about how good his game must have been. She wanted to confront her but Char was still a little girl and she didn't want to have to catch a case.

"Girl… she a mess." Brandy shook her head.

"I thought that was your baby."

"She is but when Daniel around—child please."

Pat shook her head. "Oh, hell no. I know you ain't fixing to say…"

"No, girl. No…well," Brandy shrugged her shoulders, "I don't know."

Brandy was a smart girl but she was insecure. The scar over her left eye was like the one on her heart—hardly healing. She had been in an accident when she was young and to her, she wasn't beautiful. She crept around with a lot of dudes but her self-esteem was in the slums. She was indeed trying to trap a baller but it was hard to do when she wasn't as flawless as all of the other thotties.

They pulled up to the mall and got out of the car. As they walked toward the entrance of the building Pat stopped in her tracks.

"What?" Brandy grabbed her arm and looked in the direction of her gaze.

"It's her." Pat whispered. "I can't."

Sasha was entering the mall, her belly sticking out. All of the anger Pat felt, rushed up to her throat. She stared at Sasha across the parking lot. Her feet starting moving before her brain could speak.

"Sasha!" she shouted.

Sasha's head turned in her direction, meeting a smock look of anger. Fury swirled around Pat.

"Sasha." She said, again, standing in front of a woman she had told most of her secrets to. "All I want to know is why? Why did you do this to me?"

"I just…"

"You slept with my man. You know how much I loved him. I trusted you. I trusted you to be my friend. I love you."

"Pat, he was so torn up when he found out you were pregnant. He was so angry that he couldn't get to Ken. We were talking about you and this whole thing and one thing led to another."

"Wait…" Pat put her hands up. "So you slept with him while I was fighting for my life?"

"It just happened." Sasha repeated.

"No… Things like this don't just happen. You had been plotting on him all of this time. Your fat ass always was jealous. I am so naïve to have trusted you around my man in the first place. You fucked your own brother in law, the

man your nieces and nephew share blood with. I should
have never put this pass you."

"Fuck? You attack me? You fucked Ken. You were
supposed to be leaving his dusty ass alone! But you're ass
was laid up and pregnant with that man's baby."

"That was something me and Gerald was supposed to
work out but no, you decided you wanted to eat my left
overs. You've got what you wanted, huh?"

"Look, Pat..." Sasha throw her hands up. "You and I go
too far back to be doing this. I want to put it behind..."

"Bitch!!!" Brandy stepped in front of Pat. "Ain't shit to
put behind y'all. You weren't thinking about her when you
were slurping on Gerald's dick." Brandy pulled Pat by the
arm and into the mall.

Chapter 17

Pat leaned over the toilet and threw up for the second time that morning. She hadn't slept at all the night before. Tossing and turning, thinking about Gerald and his baby with Sasha. When she saw her the day before, she felt sorry all over again. She hated the fact that her good thing had gone away.

Her phone was ringing on the sink. She wiped her mouth and reached for it. It didn't surprise her that Gerald's phone number was flashing on the screen.

"What?" Pat gagged. "What in the hell do you want?"

"You. Baby, I want you."

"Gerald you got a baby on the way." She reminded him.

"I know Pat." Gerald sighed into the phone.

"You think I'm cool with that?"

"I know you not, bae. You got to understand that I never meant for any of this happen. She was there, talking to me, consoling me while you were in the hospital. It just happened."

Pat leaned against the toilet and put her hand on her head. "Oh my god!" she shouted in frustration. "I cannot do this bullshit with you right now!" she slammed down the phone.

This cannot be life. A few weeks ago, she would have been head over heels with the way she was feeling but now, she hated the fucking ground Gerald walked on. Her phone rang again and she slid it across the room. "I hate his ass!" she shouted, tears falling down her cheeks.

This is some straight bullshit, Pat pulled herself from the floor and grabbed her phone. She couldn't believe that it was happening. She had always dreamed to be married by now. She was almost there. She almost snatched her happiness and then, he had to go fuck her friend. When she was a little girl, she would tie blankets around her body and swirl around as if it was her wedding day. She hoped that a prince would come rescue her in a horse and carriage. She would imagine doves flying around and trumpets playing. She wanted the fairytale wedding, you know that one from that Tyler Perry movie? Gerald had ruined all of that for her.

She got into her car and raced to the CVS. Her hands were shaking as she walked down the Family Planning aisle. She picked up the new test they have been advertising on TV, the one that had Bluetooth technology. It had to be accurate for twenty- nine ninety-nine. She hurried up and paid, then hopped back into the car.

As she sat down on the edge of the toilet seat, her stomach was in knots. All she could think about is being pregnant at the same time as Sasha with the same man's baby. She was utterly disgusted. She peed on the stick and waited. That was the longest two minutes of her life.

"Oh my mother fucking God!" Pat screeched. "What? I can't believe this."

She grabbed her phone and called Brandy. "Bitch…. Bitch, you ain't going to believe this hot shit." she exclaimed.

"What?" Brandy sat up in bed. "What's the matter?"

"Girl…" Pat hesitated but she had to tell someone. "I am preg…"

"Oh hell no!" Brandy shouted. "No, you not. Pat stop lying."

"Yes, bitch." Pat stared at the test. "I am pregnant."

"I cannot believe this shit." Brandy rolled Daniel over and climbed out of the bed. "I'm about to come over there." She hung up.

When Brandy came, she had a bag full of test. She sat there and watched Pat piss on all of them and they each said positive. The two of them jumped up and down for several minutes until a ton of feelings washed over Pat.

"Oh my God. Girl what's wrong?" Brandy asked as Pat plopped on the couch.

"I cannot believe this." Tears washed over her.

Brandy went to get a tub of ice cream from the freezer. She found a chick flick on Netflix and watched it as they both cried. Brandy was crying for no damn reason and Pat was crying because that's all she could do.

How in the hell was she going to tell Gerald? He was the last person she wanted to see. She didn't know what to do. She was absolutely lost.

"I can't do it." She blurted out as the credits rolled up on the television.

"Do what?"

"Have his baby." Pat looked at Brandy.

Brandy shifted her body in the chair. She put her hand on Pat's arm and as she rubbed it, the tears started all over again. She wrapped her arms around her friend and rocked her. Pat sobbed until she fell asleep.

Chapter 18

4 Months Later

Someone was pressing hard on Patricia's bell. She ran down the steps and snatched the door open. She had been waiting for a package.

"You're right on time," she said, reaching into her purse.

The man cleared his throat and she looked up. Her face dropped on the damn the floor and suddenly she was feeling sick.

"What are you doing here?"

"Baby, let me tell you…"

"What? Let you tell me what? That you want my life to be a living hell?" Pat narrowed in on him. "You tried to kill me."

"No, I didn't." he reached to touch her but she backed up.

"It wasn't me. It was Angela."

Pat smacked him. "You let her. You let her veer me off the road. You son of a bitch! I loved you. What did I do wrong, huh? You were a married man. A married man, Ken."

"I know and trust me, I am sorry."

"Get away! Get away from me, from my house!" she screamed, slamming the door in his face.

How dare he show up here, at my house? He was the very last person I wanted to see. He had cost me a loss I could never get back—one I didn't know I had but I miss it. I would have been a great mother to that baby but the chance was stolen. I still cry. I cry for my lost child. Pat cried as she sat in the kitchen.

These days, she was full of emotions. She was rattled with fear and resentment. She wanted to be mad at Ken but she couldn't. Pat was angry with herself. She allowed him to treat her the way he did. She dealt with all of his drunken nights and knew that he was no good but she loved him.

Night was falling and Pat was starting to get sleepy. It was the same exact routine every night. She would sit in front of the television and screen calls. First he would call the house phone and then, her cell. He would leave messages and even cry at times.

Her phone rang again but this time it was Brandy.

"Hello"

"Pat What are you and my niece doing?"

"We're just chilling dodging her daddy phone calls." She rubbed her stomach.

"So what are you gone do about the whole situation? I mean you'll be having your baby in a couple months and he doesn't even know your pregnant."

"I know and I plan to keep it that way. I mean, sometimes I be wanting to answer and just blurt it out like you're having a daughter but I can't. It's too much to deal with I mean this amazing man betrayed me. How can I look him in the eyes?"

"I feel you and you know we got your back," said Brandy as she smiled.

"We? I know you not talking about Sasha."

"Hell no!" Brandy snapped. "Calm down before you get my niece all worked up. I'm talking about me and my..." she paused, "fiancé." She screamed through the phone. Before Pat had the chance to congratulate her best friend, someone knocked on her door. What the hell, she thought. Is this Punk Patricia Day? Gerald's ass was standing on her porch with flowers in his hands. It had been months since they talked. She only knew that Sasha had given birth through Brandy. They haven't had a DNA test so he doesn't even know if the baby is his.

"Brandy?" Pat said.

"Yeah, girl?"

"Oh my goodness. Gerald is knocking at the door."

"Answer it. Wait don't answer it. Hell I don't know."

Pat took a deep breath and opened it.

"What do you want Gerald?"

"I just wanna talk. Can I come in for a minute?"

"I don't have anything to say to you. I'll call you right back Brandy," she hung up.

Gerald's facial expression changed when he saw her stomach. It was plump and round. He frowned and took a few steps back on the porch.

"So…" his eye brows rose on his forehead. "You been dipping and dodging me because you're pregnant? You carrying my seed and holding out?" he asked her.

"Come in." Pat stepped aside and let him in.

"I can't believe this shit." He snapped his teeth.

"You didn't need to know." She told him. "This is my baby."

"You're baby? So what? You planned on having our baby and not letting me be a part of his life?"

"Her life it's a girl." She rolled her eyes.

He picked her up and spun her around. "Put me down, Gerald. This changes nothing."

"What do you mean baby? This changes everything. I'm gone do everything in my power to get you back. Back with me where y'all need to be. WOW I'm gone have a daughter." He paced the floor. "I'm gone get her in the best schools. She gone be driving the most expensive cars and man her prom…"

Pat snapped her fingers. "Uhm calm down. She's not even born yet." Pat laughed.

Seeing him that excited about their child had her feeling some type of way.

"How do you feel? Do you need anything? Is the baby alright?"

"Gerald yes to all three. We're good." She smiled.

"I miss that beautiful smile. Baby, tell me what I gotta do for you to come home?" Gerald asked with sincerity in his voice.

Patricia looked down and then, raised her head, "Well you can start by helping me pick out a name for our daughter." She looked at Gerald.

"Baby come here." He hugged her. "I love you and I will never fuck up again"

"I'm still hurt and I don't honestly know if I could ever trust you. It's gone take a long time to get past this but I'm willing to try at least for our daughter's sake."

"Oh, I missed you so much." He held on to her as if she's trying to get loose. "Everything I did to get you, I'm gone do ten times to show you I love you and will never hurt you again."

He reached in his pocket and slips the ring on her finger. She looked at him and he said, "You never know when you might need it."

She kissed him as the tears fell from her eyes. "We'll get through this baby I promise and I know you're not ready to just pick up where we left off but I would feel much better if you moved back in with me. After all, I gotta daughter to protect, too."

"Yes, you're right. I'm not really ready to just pick up where we left off but I'm willing to start fresh and work on healing."

"Ok, I can work with that. Whatever I gotta do baby; I'll do."

"Alright, now, that we got that out the way what's up with your baby mama?"

"Man, that ain't my baby." He waved his hand. "You know she was a hoe."

"That didn't stop you from fucking her though."

"You right." He lowered his head. "I fucked her, it's over. Now, can we move on."

"Well it's getting late." Pat yawned. "Let me think on a few things and I'll call you later ok?"

"Yeah that's cool baby I'm just glad we had this time." He kissed her lips then headed out the door.

"Alright my plan is in motion all I gotta do is ride this out. I got my man and sooner than later I'll have everything that I want there's just one thing standing in my way."

So a couple days had passed by. Gerald had arranged to have Pat's things moved back to the house and she was at home settled.

Patricia decided to call Brandy but ironically Brandy was calling her.

"Hello."

"Pat, I need to talk to you."

"Girl, I was just calling you what's going on?"

"I don't know how to tell you this cause she's probably the last person in the world you wanna talk about."

"If it's about Sasha, you're absolutely correct." Pat put her hand on her hip.

"Well, there's something Gerald needs to know."

Patricia was all ears then. "About?"

"Well..." Brandy hesitated.

"Spit it out."

"The baby died." Brandy blurted out.

Pat was silent. She stood there with her hand over her mouth.

"Oh my god! I have to tell G." She said. "I'll call you back."

"But wait..." Brandy called out.

"Yea?"

"She died of SID's, at least that's what Sasha told me."

"What do you mean?"

"Well, you know, my cousin does Sasha hair and she was telling me that Sasha said the baby wasn't Gerald's. He been giving her all this money but since y'all been back together, he done cut her loose."

"I know you ain't saying what I think you saying."

"You ain't heard it from me." Brandy told her.

Even though Brandy had her doubts, she decided to take her petty hat off and go see Sasha. She was once her very good friend and she knew how hard all of this must have been on her. The baby was only a month old, but it was still her baby. Sasha opened the door before she could ring the doorbell.

"Hey, what are you doing here?" She was shocked.

"I wanted to see how you were doing." Brandy wrapped her in a hug.

They went into the living room. There was a tray of food lying out on the table and a couple of wine glasses. Brandy frowned as she sat down on the couch.

"Well, were you expecting someone?" She asked.

"People have been coming by all day since I announced her death on facebook."

Brandy's face damn neared dropped. That was tacky ass fuck but Sasha had always been an attention whore. This isn't the place or time, though.

"I am so sorry." Brandy said again. "She was beautiful."

"Wasn't she?" Sasha smiled but it seemed so fake.

She was hiding something, Brandy knew it. The entire aura of the room was completely off. Something sinister was going on. Sasha didn't act like she was in mourning of the only person who had heard her heart beat from the inside. She didn't look like she had cried at all.

"Have you told Pat?" Her eyes darted at Brandy.

Brandy cleared her throat. "Yes, I told her."

"I'm sure she'll tell Gerald." A smile crept on to her face.

"Is this some type of fucking game to you?" Brandy flipped. "You over there laughing and your baby just died."

"Don't you think I fucking know that? I know she's dead. I know I will never hear her cry again. I guess its karma, huh? Where this hell is Gerald? He is supposed to be here." She suddenly started to cry.

Even though she doesn't condone what happened she felt bad for her situation "Why Gerald? Of all the men in the world why him?"

Sasha tried to fight back the tears, "You don't understand."

"Well help me understand then cause that was some fucked up shit to go behind her back and sleep with her man. Now let's be real here we been rocking together for years and you gone risk that over some dick? Come on. Now. Pat has been there for you she was like your sister and you played her like this? Shit is unforgiveable."

Sasha stood and wiped the tears from her face.

"Oh so during my time of need you wanna scold me for Pat? You know what? Just get out!" Sasha shouted.

Gerald slipped into the bed behind Pat, and wrapped his arms around her. She turned and kissed him on the lips.

"Have you heard?"

"Heard what?"

"The baby died."

"What? What baby?" he patted her stomach.

"Sasha's baby. You're baby. How come you didn't know?"

"What? That's so sad. When I found out the baby wasn't mine, I blocked her on my phone. She couldn't call me. I feel sorry for her though." He said nonchalantly.

Chapter 19

"What the fuck took so long?" Angela snatched the door open.

"I had to nestle my honey," G kissed her.

"Fuck out of here," she laughed. "I thought my girl was much smarter than this."

"Yea, me too but we got business to talk about." G sat down on the couch and pulled out a blunt. "You puffing?"

"Nah." Angela sat across from him. "I got the rest of the money. How much longer this shit going to take? You over there trying to wife the bitch and shit."

"That's why I need to talk to you." He told her.

Angela frowned knowing he was about to tell her some bullshit. She held her breath.

"I don't need the rest of the money. I'm calling it off."

"You can't do that." She started talking some shit in Spanish. "I paid you."

"Look, I love her."

"Love? You fucking idiot. You don't know shit about love." She yelled. "Kill the bitch! That was your only fucking job! What the fuck is wrong with you?"

"You on some bullshit. She's having my baby."

"So were them other bitches."

Gerald puffed his blunt and blew a circle in the air. He was out of the deal. If Angela wanted Pat dead, she would have to do it herself. He pulled a wad out of his pocket and put it on the table.

"It's over."

Patricia was jolted from her sleep by the vibrating of her cell phone. She frowned when the name Kenneth Ross flashed on the screen.

"This must be some type of sick joke and the shit ain't funny."

The phone stopped ringing, then rung again. She was afraid to answer it but took a deep breath and said, "Hello?"

"Patricia, baby it feels so good to hear your voice."

"I don't know what kind of sick freak you are but I'm hanging up." She was interrupted.

"Patricia, please don't hang up. It's me Ken and before you cuss me out, I can explain everything."

Pat was so caught off guard by this she sat up in disbelief. Could this really be him? I mean how and he's dead who is this?

"Pat, it's Ken."

"Prove it, then."

"The last time me and you made love it was at your house. We listened to Luther Vandross until we fell asleep. The next morning you kicked me out but you told me you loved me."

There was a moment of silence then tears started falling from her eyes.

"OMG! Ken I thought you were dead."

"Yeah so did a lot of people and that was the plan. Pat I need to see you. Can you meet me right now?"

"Of course I can. Where?"

He gave her all the details as to where to meet him and call once she was close.

"I'm on my way." She wiped the tears away—more fell as she cried. She also laughed with joy. "

I gotta tell Brandy. No he said don't tell anybody."

She pulled up and knocked on the door. He looked through the peep hole and sees her standing there. He quickly opened the door and snatched her in. He hugged her so tight and kissed her forehead.

"Let me look at you"

She hit him and yelled, "How come you had me thinking you were dead?" She broke down crying.

"Baby hurting you was the last thing I ever wanted to do but at the time I had no other choice. Your life was in danger, too that's why I couldn't contact you. Baby I need to tell you something and I need you to listen."

"Ok," She said hesitantly.

"Gerald isn't who you think he is."

Pat pulled away from him, smacking her lips. "What are you talking about? Gerald isn't who he says he is?"

"I know all of this is going to sound crazy to you but I'm telling you the truth."

"Truth? This is coming from a dead man though. I know you ain't bring me here just to get me caught up in your scams I knew this was a bad idea." She headed toward the door. Ken had to do something to stop her from leaving so he blurts out,

"He was hired to kill you."

She stopped and turned around, "What did you just say?"

"I said Gerald was hired to kill you."

"Now I know you're delusional," she frowned. "Gerald loves me. We're getting married and starting our own family. Why would he want to kill me?"

"Pat sit down please let me explain. When I went to confront Angela, she was drunk and venting. She confessed about hiring someone to kill you. It just so happened to be you're beloved Gerald."

"You're lying. Gerald loves me he would never hurt me let alone try and kill me."

"Why do you think every time something happened he was able to get to you so fast? No matter where he was at he would always be the first one there, now why is that? Not to mention not one police officer was ever called for any of those incidents."

"That doesn't mean nothing."

"Come on baby your smarter than that. You gotta trust me. This is life or death here." Patricia got up and headed for the door again.

"I don't believe you."

"Just wait until Detective Collins talks to you you'll believe me then."

"Who is Detective Collins?"

"The lead detective working this homicide case."

"Homicide?" She asked with a shocked look on her face.

"Yes that's what I've been trying to tell you. He's not who he said he is. I bet you didn't know he had a woman pregnant before you that was no longer seen or heard from."

"Ok people break up and move on just like I'm bout to do right now." She headed for the door again.

"Patricia if you walk out that door you're gonna be sorry."

She slammed it behind her.

"Damn."

On the drive home Pat started thinking about all that was said.

"Ken is a liar. I'm not believing nothing that came out of his lying mouth. He's just trying to break us up and take the blame off his psychotic ass wife."

Pat's phone rang and it was Brandy.

"Hello."

"Hey girl. How's my niece? What the doctor say?"

"She's good. He wants me to take it easy cause he doesn't think I'm going to make my due date." She sighed.

"What's all that for?"

"Me and Ken just lightweight got into it."

"Ken?" Brandy looked at the phone in her hand.

"Pat, are you ok cause last time I checked Ken had died, baby."

"It's a long story. I'm headed your way now."

"Ok."

Brandy opened the door just as Pat got to it. "Hurry up and tell me what's going on because I can't believe this shit."

"Ok, when I left the doctor's he called me and at first I thought somebody was playing so I had him prove it. Then once he did that he asked me to meet him so he could explain what was going on. I get there and he's going on about how Angela hired Gerald to kill me."

"Whaaat? Nah, I don't believe that."

"Same thing I said but he insisted he's telling the truth that Gerald was the one that tried to kill him that night but he shot someone else. That before me, he had gotten another woman pregnant and she hasn't been seen or heard from since."

"That doesn't mean nothing."

"Same thing I said like people break up and move on."

"Right."

"Oh and another thing he mentioned, every time something happened with me Gerald was always the first to be there before anybody and never once were police called out."

"That just mean he was always there. Pat you must be going crazy right now. To find out Ken is still alive and he's accusing Gerald of trying to kill you. Well forget all of that I know it's easier said than done but you need to take a nice hot bath and relax. Do you wanna chill here?"

"Nah, I'm not scared to go home." They laughed.

"I'll be alright. I'm bout to go home and lay down and utilize Nadia's services."

Pat headed for the door. Brandy gave her a hug. "Call me later."

"Ok."

When Pat arrived home Gerald is there waiting for her. "Hey baby. Is everything alright?"

He tried to touch her but she shies away. "Yeah I'm just tired. Doctor said I should take it easy because he doesn't think I'll go to my due date."

"Ok so in other in other words, you're on bedrest?"

"No he just said try and stay off my feet as much as possible, no heavy lifting and come back if my contractions get like two to three minutes apart."

"Are you dilated? Did they check your cervix?"

"Look at you sounding like a pro. You sure you haven't done this before? You sure you don't have any babies running around out here?"

"Nah, baby I told you you're the only one." He told her as she thought back on what Ken said. "I love you."

"I love you too, Gerald."

Chapter 20

"Hello"

"Hello, is Patricia Davis available?"

"Who's calling?"

"This is Detective Collins with the homicide division."

"This is she. How can I help you?"

"I was wondering if we could meet today to go over a few things?"

"What kind of things? What is this about?"

"I would rather not discuss this over the phone. Is it possible to meet me?"

"Ok where?"

"Same place you went yesterday."

"Ok. I can be there in about an hour."

"Ok, see you in an hour."

"Impossible there can't be any truth to this there just can't be," Pat thought aloud as she hugged her stomach and cried. "I'm so happy right now and everything could be falling apart. What if he was hired to kill me? What am I gone do? Stop it Pat he loves the ground you walk on and is so excited about his daughter this is a big mistake."

She got herself together. Nadia passed her in the hallway. "Hello Ms. Patricia. Can I get you anything to eat?"

"Oh, no, thank you, Nadia. I already have butterflies in my stomach but thank you anyway."

She headed on out to meet with the detective and find out what's going on. Pat reached the motel and knocked on the door. When the door opened there stood an older gentleman salt and pepper hair nice trimmed mustache wearing a suit and visible evidence that he loved donuts. "Hello you must be Patricia. Nice to meet you. I'm Detective Collins." He flashed his badge.

She gave him a fake smile as she walked through the door. "Ok, Patricia. the reason I brought you here is because it seems as though your mixed up in some serious shit—excuse my language."

"But I haven't done anything."

"And I'm not saying you did just hear me out. You're boyfriend is a very dangerous man. Did you know that?"

"No and he hasn't proven that to me either. He's one of the sweetest men I've ever met."

"Ok," He opened up a manila folder and starts laying pictures out.

"Now did you know that he was capable of doing this?"

She gasped and covered her mouth. "No, Gerald didn't do this. He couldn't have. He's not that type of guy."

"Alright Patricia since you know him so well and know his type, do you know what your man does for a living?"

"Yes I do. He owns a couple nightclubs and some other property."

"Alright you know a little bit of his front spots but your man is a dope boy and he's also a hitman for hire."

Pat looked at him, "Hitman for hire? What does that mean?"

"It means if you want someone to disappear and you got the money he can make it happen. Let me ask you a question are you aware of his last relationship?"

"I knew of her I mean I didn't know she was pregnant. I know they were supposed to had broken up and she left."

"Well rumor has it he killed her."

"Killed her? Why would he kill her?"

"She knew too much. She had come to me when she first witnessed him kill a man. She said she feared for her life and the safety of her unborn child. Word had gotten back to Gerald and ever since then no one has seen or heard from her. Neighbors say they heard screaming coming from the house on the night of and the next day Gerald said she had left. There was no sign of foul play or a struggle so we couldn't run him in but the years went by and the case went cold until we stumbled upon Ken. He told us everything that happened. how Gerald tried to kill him and how he was hired by his wife to kill you so we've been back on his ass. He won't get away with it this time."

"I can't bring myself to believe any of this it's all so unbelievable." She broke down. Ken grabbed her some tissue and tried to comfort her.

"I know this is a lot to take in Pat but if you never trust me on anything else in you're life please trust me on this. I'm worried about you and just want you to be safe." He held her hand.

"I just don't understand none of this. I mean you both are telling me that my fiancé, my daughter's father wants to kill me. Yes, it's a lot to take in at once, but I'm fine. I don't feel like I'm in any danger. I appreciate you telling me this but I need some time to think." She grabbed her things.

"Patricia baby please don't go back there. Please don't go back to that man."

"That man is my fiancé and I love him and he wouldn't hurt me."

"You're not gone be satisfied until he kills you and your daughter huh?" Ken yelled at her.

Patricia looked back at him shaking her head as she walked out the door. "Damn I shouldn't have said that." he punched the wall.

"No you told her right. Don't worry. I'll put a car on her just in case."

Patricia cried the whole drive back. She called Brandy. "Hello"

"Brandy it's all true it's all fucking true. Gerald was paid by Angela to kill me. They think he killed his last girlfriend and she was pregnant, Brandy."

"OMG Pat! Where are you now?"

"Just leaving from there on my way home to confront this son of a bitch."

"Pat listen to me that is not a good idea." She started putting her shoes on.

"I don't know what the fuck is going on all I know is the bullshit stops now. My daughter will not lose her life or her mommy. I promise you that" She hung up the phone.

"Pat." Brandy calls out her name. "Oh no I gotta hurry and get over there!"

Brandy raced to Gerald's place. She kept trying to call Pat's cell phone but it was going straight to voicemail. Patricia finally pulled in the driveway jumped out of the car and stormed inside. Gerald was waiting for her in the bedroom little did he know the wait was over. She opened the door with tears down her face and fire in her eyes.

"What's wrong baby?"

"Oh now I'm baby huh?"

"What you mean? I've always called you my baby."

"Ok Gerald well answer me this do you love me?"

"Of course I love you. What's going on?"

"You tell me cause the way I hear it you were hired to kill me."

Gerald's eyes got big.

"Now wait a minute Patricia I can explain everything."

"Explain? What is there to explain? Angela hired you and you were planning on killing me point blank period no explanations needed."

"You got it all wrong let me explain." He walked toward her. She reached down in her purse and pointed a gun at him.

"Don't come near me you son of a bitch. I don't trust you and therefore I will shoot you if you come any closer."

He stepped back and took a seat. "Baby, yes Angela hired me to do a job for her she said she wanted this woman gone and that's all I knew. In my line of work, you don't ask questions you're paid to do a job."

"So I was a job?" She chuckled and shook her head. "

In the beginning when she first hired me, but I had no idea I would fall in love with you. That first night I saw you at the club I knew I couldn't go through with it you were just so beautiful. That's why she kept calling you with the private messages trying to scare you away from me so that I couldn't protect you."

"Protect me hell you were the one trying to kill me. I should've had protection from you're ass."

"I took care of her Patricia. She was the one trying to kill you. After I gave her back her money and told her that I wasn't gone go through with it she hired someone else. She was just so persistent in getting rid of you. I couldn't come out and tell you that it wasn't a coincidence that we met that night. What was I gone say? Hey I've been hired to kill you, but would you like to go out with me anyway? Naw I knew that night when I saw you at the club you were too beautiful for anyone to hurt. I wanted nothing more than to wake up to your smile everyday why you think I worked so hard to keep you baby? I love you."

Patricia is slowly breaking down "I don't believe a word that's coming out of your mouth. I can't believe after all this time I was so blind for you." She rubbed her stomach. "I can't believe I'm having your child." She kneeled on the floor. "OMG!"

"Are you in labor?" He came closer and she pointed the gun at him again.

"Don't touch me. Don't come near me." She cried from the pain.

Just then, Brandy comes in the room and saw Pat holding the gun and crying in pain. From the way Pat is kneeling Brandy knows she's going into labor.

"Pat put down the gun. I know what you're going through, but he's not worth it. We gotta get you to the hospital you're going into labor."

"No, I'm not leaving yet until he admits everything."

"What else do you want me to say Pat? The bitch hired me but I quit! I fucking quit! Our baby is coming. We have to go."

"Fuck you! You don't have a daughter and I hope you spend the rest of your miserable life behind bars. Did you think I was gone be like your last girlfriend? Uh uh I wasn't giving you the chance to hurt me again. I can't believe I fell for all you're lies the bullshit was convincing but it ends today. I hope you had a nice laugh cause the jokes on you."

"What is that supposed to mean?" He walked closer to her and she fired and hit him in the chest.

She gasped, "oh my God Gerald! I'm so sorry what have I done?"

Brandy took the gun out of her hands and hugged her tight "It's gone be alright, Pat. I got you."

Gerald laid there bleeding out. Nadia comes to the doorway along with a couple officers that were following Patricia.

"I heard the shot when I was talking to the detectives at the door and we came running to see what had happened. I'm so glad you're alright Ms. Patricia." she whispered in her ear. Brandy was doing her best to try and calm Pat down, but between what had just taken place and the fact that she was in labor she was an emotional wreck. The detectives had called for an ambulance and the coroner to come to Gerald's house. Word had gotten back to Detective Collins and Ken about the shooting and that Pat was taken to the hospital. There was no way anyone was keeping Ken from going and checking up on Pat case or no case that was his heart. By the time Ken and Detective Collins reached the hospital Pat had given birth to her daughter, Brandy. She thought it was only right to name her after her sister who had been there through it all.

Made in the USA
Columbia, SC
16 June 2018